*The
Summer
of the
Falcon*

The
Summer
of the
Falcon

By Jean Craighead George

Illustrated by the Author

THOMAS Y. CROWELL COMPANY   NEW YORK

TO JOHN M. ALLEN
who uncovered the story of the falcon
and made me write it, tears or no tears.

Designed by Albert Burkhardt
Manufactured in the United States of America
Library of Congress Catalog Card No. 62-16543
ISBN 0-690-79269-7
6 7 8 9 10

Contents

I . Pritchard's

June burst through the big walnut doors and ran up the dark stairs to her room. With a hoot she pushed up the window, stood on one foot, and kicked back the shutters. Quickly, before it was all gone, she threw open the closet and smelled the mysterious scent of the bats which had been hanging upside down in the corners all winter. She slid open the bureau drawer and sniffed the too sweet dust of the winter-working, wood-boring beetle. Then she closed her eyes and took in every musty smell, for they told her the routines of winter were done and the summer was beginning.

Downstairs windows were being hiked—long shoves that brought the sashes to the ceiling in that Victorian house. Tight doors were being shouldered ajar, and the sun and fresh air were racing into the tall rooms and dark corridors. Summer came pouring in, and the mysterious smells of a house locked for nine months blew out, clearing June's head of school.

From her room that looked across the creek she could hear suitcases banging up the walnut staircases and sheets being snapped over beds.

The house was big and gray and sat far out in the country along a dirt road that followed the Yellow Breeches Creek from the Blue Mountains to Boiling Springs. A one-track railroad ran nearby. The house had been built by June's grandfather for his bride and was an expression of his love. It sang out with the best of its day: rococo trim on pointed eaves, whirligigs on the windows, wooden flowers and leaves on the overhang of the porches—yards of Victorian ginger-bread. Green lawns spread out around the house. The creek, wide, and deep enough for swimming, ran past the back porch.

June and her twin brothers knew it was the most beautiful house in the world. Whatever its oddities and drawbacks they did not see them. It glowed in their minds, for here they ran barefooted through rooms, up and down stairs and over the meadows and fields until their mother gathered them in in September and took them back to the city and the dark months of school.

The house was to have been sold after Grandfather Pritchard's death. It might have been, had not June's mother looked at the stream, the mountains, the vaulting rooms, and asked that it be kept for the Pritchard children so that they might have a sense of their past by playing on the land their ancestors opened.

Then, knowing other members of her husband's family would share the house, she said, "and each wife will have her own table, stove, and refrigerator, so the women will not squabble."

June stepped neatly out of her shoes. Last year she had kicked them off. She chuckled at the memory of how young she had been to do that. One grows a lot in a year, she said to herself as she placed the shoes under the bed. She unpacked her shorts and shirts and dresses and library books. As she arranged her clothes, a mouse in the top drawer circled nervously in its nesting material of old newspapers and mattress stuffings. June did not bother to remove it; each summer a mouse was there, and each summer, annoyed by the opening and closing of the drawers, it eventually moved off to the quieter interiors of walls and floors and wainscotings. Nature had a way, the children learned at Pritchard's, of accommodating itself to the comings-and-goings of human beings.

June closed her eyes and heard the creek rushing over the milldam. She could hold the happiness no longer. She ran: out her door, down the back steps—two at a time—over the porch, across the yard to the stream. Gathering speed, she jumped off the end of the canoe landing, sailed through the air, and grasped the tree-tied rope. She swung out, kicking, and looked into the green water. She swung back over the land and saw the grass and stones. And she almost hit Rod as he came out of the creek beside the sycamore roots.

"Hi!" he said with an open smile. June dropped onto the grass. Rod sat down beside her. Rod was her cousin, twelve years old. He had tight, curly hair, wide-set brown eyes, and angular knees and elbows. All the Pritchard men were wiry, but Rod was knotty.

He was the most imaginative person she had ever known, and could quickly bring her to anger or laughter as they struggled to live in a friendly way, side by side.

Rod always started the summers nicely. This year he said, "Junie, let's be friends every single day this year. Even on the day we go home."

June's blue eyes stared into Rod's brown ones as she remembered the parting last summer—fisticuffs and tears. She said, "Are you sure you mean it?"

"Toe four jays!" he answered. She had almost forgotten their private language. Some of their friends spoke pig-Latin or had secret passwords to hold them together, but Rod had outdone them all. He had created a whole new language, complete with verbs, nouns, adjectives, adverbs. He had taught it to June, and she had loved it with envious jealousy, because she so wished she had invented it. "Feet squawl," was the verb "to be." It was declined, "toe squal, heel squil, knee squad (I am, you are, he is)."

As June remembered, she slowly translated "Toe four jays." Rod had said, "I promise forever." Her heart warmed. She laughed. Summer and good fellowship filled her. "All right," she said. "Let's be good friends!"

Rod squinted down on his white toes that had just escaped shoes, and added, "I also promise I won't smash the next city of Clayforbia we build."

The city of Clayforbia had begun the day they had discovered a bank of clay in the bend of the creek. They had dug out a bucket of the white slippery earth and shaped it. Rod had made a house. He'd placed it on the bank. June had drawn a road beside it with a stick and had made a neighboring house. Then, street by street, a city had emerged along the banks of the creek as they duplicated the world into which they were growing. Other boys they knew built small railroads, the girls played "house," even June's brothers at her age had hollowed out a tree in which they cooked and slept—but Rod and June had a city.

Late in the summer Rod and June began to bicker, then to tease, and finally to fight, not about anything, really, but the squabbling seemed imperative. Finally June got so angry she hid Rod's bathing suit on a hot summer noon and climbed onto the porch roof where he could not find her. Rod called, looked for her, grew angry. Then he ran to the creek with a croquet mallet and smashed Clayforbia to dust. June saw him from up high. Slowly she came down from the rooftop and walked to the city. Rod stood in the ruins staring at her. The mallet fell from his hand as he stomped away.

So last summer had ended. Now a new one was beginning.

June walked toward the canoe landing. "I don't think I want to build a Clayforbia this year."

"Why not?" he asked.

"Well, I'm in my teens now, thirteen. And I feel differently about some things."

"You do?" he said in awe. "Like what?"

"Well . . ." she floundered, "well, I must sit nicely now, not hunch over. And I must speak in a low, refined voice, not scream, and . . ." She could hear her mother's voice telling her the new rules. She could still see her bedroom door swinging closed, feel the warm air, and feel the indignation as she was told how to behave, not like a child any longer, but like a woman. The only thing that made this bearable was the knowledge that her brothers had been given a "growing-up" lecture by her father, that most of her friends had begun to "learn the rules." But to June the rules seemed unreal—and unfair.

Rod came toward her with blotter-interest. "Are you getting to be a lady or something?" he asked. She spun off and ran over the railroad tracks and down the cow path into the meadow. She wished for someone to talk to, someone or something that would listen to the loneliness of her confusion.

Rod followed her over the tracks. "Do you suppose, Junie," he called tentatively, "that this all has something to do with having babies?"

"Go away," she screamed in rage. "Go far, far away. You're just awful." Rod shrugged and turned back. She heard his toes crunch the cinders on the railbed, then his legs catapulted him back to the house. He seemed so free as he ran. Boys were lucky; they could do what they wanted. They also got the exciting things to do, like lawn mowers. Girls got the dull chores, like weeding.

She waded into the creek to watch a water strider fight the current to stand still. Suddenly her foot struck slickness and she reached down to find a new supply of clay. Her anger left. She thought of clay houses and stores, and the cozy walls of Clayforbia.

And then her mother called. June could see a yellow dress shining through the marshmallow bushes as the voice came from the back porch. "Juunieee."

She called again, "Juuniee!"

June hummed defiantly.

Then came a louder call—her brother Don. "June, where are you? We have something for you!"

June splashed out of the water and ran toward the house. The family was clustered on the porch. There were her brothers, Don and Charles, and her cousins, Jim and Rod; Uncle Paul and Aunt Helen, her mother and her father— all peering at something in a bushel basket. June slowed to a walk and crossed her fingers. She had been promised a pet this summer and her family was smiling as if this were the moment. She whispered Rod's secret language, "Lee, prod bennet squawl spid et gill." Translated, "Oh, please let it be alive and young."

In the basket, braced on a stub of a tail, was a robin-sized sparrow hawk, North America's smallest falcon.

Her hands cupped the screaming bird and she lifted it to her cheek. A blue talon dug her hand, the other clenched her shirt. The falcon was afraid, and he clung tighter and tighter. June held it close, for she knew that all young life is scared and unsure.

Don gently pried the claws from the blouse, wrapped his

palm around its feet, and presented her with the bird.

"Here is a lady's falcon, for a lady," he said.

She again took the screaming baby of the wild in her hands. The bird stopped fighting and chirped softly.

June placed him deep in the basket, but as she released him, he shot out a blue foot, broke the skin of her hand, and screamed in rage.

"Fierce King Alexander," she said. "His name has got to be Zander."

Her brother Charles smiled in approval. "Soon we'll 'jesse' him and start his training," then sternly, "and get yourself in a work mood . . . training a falcon is tedious and demanding."

Her father raised one eyebrow as he looked into the basket. At times his rigid rules made June sad. She could not always fit them. At other times his rules were the shield she seemed to need. Now she tried not to hear him. "June, you must take daily care of that bird. You're tending a bit of life. It will be totally dependent upon you for its comfort and existence. If you're going to neglect it, let it go."

June ached inside as her mother prolonged the dictum. "That's one thing my husband will not tolerate," she said to Aunt Helen, "neglect of an animal. I surely hope June sticks to this. She does have her head in the clouds so much of the time."

An hour ago the words would have hurt, but now, as June lifted the dusty bird again, she felt enormous and strong. She studied the falcon in wonderment. He was beautiful and alive . . . and hers! He was the first thing she had ever owned completely, and she had a sense of

wealth and richness. She trembled to possess such an exquisite thing.

Slowly the porch cleared, the excitement died down and
June was alone with her possession. She whispered to the
bird, "Dear falcon Zander, you have been taken from your
mother, from the freedom of the open sky and the wind
and clouds . . . but I shall replace them all with my love."
And she stroked him. He bit her finger. It hurt, for the
beak was powerful, but she only winced. "You're going to
have to learn the rules, little fellow. And when you've
learned them, then I can let you play free." She held the
falcon close. "They've told me a million times that when
all the rules are learned and buried in habit, freedom begins.
So you'll have to learn the rules, too."

Once more she put the bird down. The wind stirred
across the porch and dipped into the basket. It lifted a
wisp from the immature head and took it circling out and
up. June watched the feather blow over the yard and vanish
in the bigness of the trees and sky. When she looked again
at the falcon, his cap was a little redder where a new feather
showed.

2. *The Jesses*

The next day June climbed from the brass bed before dawn and knelt beside the basket. The bird was wide awake. His brown eyes fastened on her movements. His blue beak dropped open from the bottom and he sat defensively on his tail. Carefully June touched his stroobly head, and was surprised to discover that the feathers were warm.

Again the blue talons grabbed her. She pulled away, but the screaming bird came flapping along, his talons deep in her hand. He fluttered, let go, and dropped on the bed. Flipping to his back he threw both feet in the air—the reaction of a cornered bird of prey. As June moved back,

Zander jumped to his feet, and, too young to fly, lifted his wings and ran across the covers. At the edge of the bed, as if at the edge of the nest, he tidily defecated. June tidily cleaned up.

That done, the falcon let her pick him up and place him in the basket, where he watched as she slipped into her clothes, frightened by every grossly human movement she made. She chattered to him as she dressed. "Your mother was much daintier and smaller than I am, wasn't she?"

Then June tiptoed to the door and quietly closed it behind her.

She stole past the bedroom where her parents were sleeping and paused at the bathroom door to listen to the honey-bees in the south wall of the house. They entered through a small hole under the bathroom window. Occasionally they got mixed up and came inside—to the concern of people *and* bees. But rarely did they sting. So they were not removed from the walls but were left, like the mice in the drawer, to tolerate the people in summer and assume their rightful ownership of the house when the people were gone.

As June listened to the bees she wondered if she should catch some in a bottle for her falcon . . . she had heard that little falcons like bees and insects. But they seemed a small, hot bite for her young falcon, and she went on with her first plan. For this she needed Jim, Rod's brother.

The boys were lined along the railing of the sleeping porch on their cots. Cousin Jim was awake the moment she opened the door. He looked at her out of strong brown eyes. Jim, like all the Pritchard males, had a deep love of the birds and beasts and fish and plants around him. In Jim this interest was so intense that it awoke him at five and propelled him into the stream and meadow, to crayfish it among the rocks and water as he searched for nests and dens.

"Jim," June whispered, "Zander is hungry. I need some sparrows. Come with me to the barn." And Jim was suddenly on the floor fully dressed. During the summer the brown, slender child rarely got into pajamas. He was so tired at night that he just fell into bed with his clothes on. When his mother complained, he put on his pajamas over his shirt and pants.

Jim poured some cold water from a pitcher into the old porcelain basin and washed his face. As he looked up he said, "Bobu is back from his hunt."

Above him on the window trim sat a small, gray screech owl. Bobu had been her brothers' pet for two years. He was so tame that the brothers had never bothered to leash him. He needed only food and affection to keep him close. He would fly away to hunt at night and return to the porch by day, going to sleep when the boys got up. "Musical beds," they called it.

Bobu had another enchanting habit: he rode the old victrola in the living room. Whenever he came into the house he would fly to the turntable and wait until someone came to wind it. Then, circling, circling, he would spin around and around, making contented owl noises, captivating everyone with his funny, swivelling head. "Wind up Bobu's amusement park," Aunt Helen would say when the owl flew into the house.

As Bobu circled his head, Jim said to him, "Where 'ya been?" and the speechless bird chuttered and closed his eyes tight.

"He looks Chinese when he sleeps," Jim observed as he lifted his hand. The quick movement awakened the half-peeking owl and he flew to the boy.

"Where's Windy?" Jim asked. Swinging softly, silently out of the dawn light came a creamy-colored barn owl. Windy made seven of Bobu, for he was a much larger species. He alighted on the railing and bobbed his head.

Four years ago the twins had found Windy at the foot of his nest tree in Rock Creek Park and had brought him home. As the funny, ugly owlet hissed and sissed, their mother had said, "You ought to call him Windy."

Each bird in the family—the falcons, the owls—had its own whistle to which it came like a dog when called, but Windy was the most obedient. When he heard his call he came home from tree hollows far away.

As June greeted the owls she wondered how Zander was going to like them. In the wild, Zander would not meet an owl, for the owls fly by night, the hawks by day. June was a little fearful for her youngest of the birds. Then the owl eyes turned softly upon her and blinked. She blinked back and whispered, "Dear Bobu, you'll like Zander. He's little, like you." The owl blinked again.

By this time Charles had awakened. "Whatcha doing?" he asked. As he moved, Fingers, the raccoon, poked his head out of the barrel under his bed and scratched.

Fingers was a wonderful pet—except that he took all the labels off tin cans, paper off walls, and slept in the sugar

barrel whenever he could. Mrs. Pritchard had relegated
him to the outdoors, saying, "There *are* limits."

June told Charles they were going to shoot sparrows in
the barn. He decided to come along. Then Don rolled over
and got up. He wasted no words. He had no need to.
June's twin brothers were so close that when one started a
sentence the other finished it. The same ideas came to
them at the same time. They had the same fillings in their
teeth, had caught the measles the same day, also the chicken
pox and mumps.

It did not matter that most people could not tell them
apart. If one was called, both came or either. They moved
as one. And they called themselves "I," never "we." And
yet, each was different.

The twins were crackling motion. As soon as they were
up, the porch was aburst with activity. Even the owls
moved and bobbed. The quick movements of the brothers
motivated boys and beasts and birds . . . all but cousin
Rod. He rolled over and went back to sleep. Bobu saw the
sleeper and flew to him without sound. As Rod mumbled
and nuzzled deeper in the covers, Bobu ran down the
mountain of blankets into the cozy hollow of the warm,
dark opening under Rod's chin. Rod grinned in his half-
sleep. The owl, accustomed to the tight closeness of hollows in the wild, enjoyed cozy contact with things and
people when in captivity. Rod hugged Bobu as a hollow
tree would.

June and the boys returned before breakfast with plenty
of fresh food for the owls and falcons. They wrapped it

carefully in waxed paper and put it in the left-hand corner of the icebox. This tolerance of fresh-killed sparrows in her domain was Elizabeth Pritchard's contribution to falconry. She believed in children with projects and she put up with the difficulties such projects might involve.

After breakfast, June proudly carried the basket with Zander to the lawn under the maple tree, where her brothers' falcons were tethered to their perches.

There were four of these noble birds at Pritchard's that summer: three Cooper's hawks and a magnificent duck hawk, the falcon of the kings. The duck hawk was called Ulysses. As large as a crow, he had enormous shoulders, a tapered, streamlined body, and velvety black patches around his black eyes. His breast was creamy rose with ebony dots; his back was slate blue and black and white, and intricately marked; each feather was edged with white. Ulysses was their great pride. But Ulysses was not a "falcon" in the king's English. He was a tiercel—a *male*. Only the bigger and more powerful *female* duck hawk could properly be called a "falcon." June had often heard her brothers say that no other bird could bear this title in the days of falconry. But nowadays Ulysses and Zander were known commonly as falcons. Their wings were distinctively pointed, their tails long. June knew them all by the names the scientists had given them and could identify them as they flew. The Cooper's hawks have long tails and short, rounded wings. The Buteos include the rough-legged hawks and the red-tails. They have broad wings and broad, rounded tails, and they soar in wide circles high in the air. Then there are the eagles. But the highest form of all are the falcons—in North America the gyrfalcon, the prairie falcon, the duck hawk, pigeon hawk, and the sparrow hawk.

She had listened sharply to her brothers when they told her what had happened to the names for birds since falconry began. She admired the regal Ulysses, but was glad for her gentler "lady's falcon," and for his daintier size which enabled her to hold him in both her hands.

Suddenly Charles ran out the back door on a trot and handed June some falcon food. "Here are some tidbits for Zander. He's still a baby so you'll have to feed him twice a day."

Don joined them. "He'll get hunger streaks the way Jess did if you don't feed him right." He pointed to his female Cooper's hawk. On her tail were three fine white lines, straight across every feather, which showed a lack of bone and viscera and other nutrients, marking the days before Don found her.

Jim's young voice interrupted them, "Aunt Roodie has teeth with marks across them. Are those people hunger streaks?"

"No," Don answered him seriously, "probably a high temperature." He slipped on his gauntlet, put his fist behind Ulysses' feet, and tapped the bird's legs. Ulysses stepped on his hand to start the morning routine of "flying" the falcons.

As June fed Zander, she watched the process closely, studying carefully the techniques of falconry she would soon be employing. A throb of excitement went through her as she watched Ulysses, tethered to a long cord, fly from the creek to the maple at the sound of three whistled notes. Don fed him small bites of food so that he would remain hungry enough to fly the distance four times. Then he gave the bird a full-course meal. Because the summertime was muggy and was poor weather for hunting, Ulysses was merely being exercised to keep him fit for the time in late August and early September when the nippy air would brighten the bird and he would hunt pheasants.

Charles was struggling with his Cooper's hawk. "Jess doesn't even want to eat today," he said as he held a meal three feet from the hawk. Jess stared at the food but would not move.

"Well, Zander is hungry," June said, and stuck a bleeding thumb in her mouth.

"That's a spunky little bird," Don observed as he brought Ulysses back to his perch. "He ought to make a good hunter—if you can ever get him whipped into line." He looked at June, knowingly. "It sure takes work and patience."

For an instant her anger rose. Then Zander fluttered in his basket and cried. She smiled and said solemnly, "I promise to do it right."

For a week June played with Zander, letting him sit on her finger or chase ants and crickets. And as she played she talked to him—a silent dialogue—in which she confessed that her mother had embarrassed her yesterday when she had flicked her skirts and kicked her heels to show Uncle Paul she could do the Charleston. She said softly, "Oh, Zander!" and sighed. The bird cocked its head at her voice, then took its yellow toe in its beak and bit it gently. June stopped talking to herself and laughed. "That's marvelous, Zander, I don't think I could bite my toe."

Twelve days later Charles touched Zander's brick-red tail feathers, which were now edged with black and white trim, and announced that the bird was full grown.

"It's time to jesse him," he said. "His fledglinghood is over; his training must begin! We'll start tomorrow."

The next morning June awoke in a bleak mood. She sought the twins on the sleeping porch. "Do we really have to jesse Zander?" she asked before they were awake enough to think.

"Of course!" came two voices. Don carried on, "It's only a falcon, not a person . . . you're always putting your feelings into the dogs and raccoons and birds. And that's not right."

Charles continued, "It's this simple. If you want a falcon, you jesse and train him. It never hurt a bird to be trained, so don't be silly about it. They're cared for. They like it!"

After drying the breakfast dishes June met the falconers on the canoe landing. She felt better.

"Training makes life easier," her mother had told her as they did the dishes. "Women learn this earlier than men because their work is all around them. Even so, it was years before my hands cooked and made beds without my mind laboring to help them." Elizabeth Pritchard lifted her hands and turned them slowly. "Now they go one way and my head another. I can even worry and work."

June was still rebellious, "Why can't women be trained to do something else? Beds and dishes are so horribly dull."

"They can," her mother answered, "but someday you will want to do these dull things for the husband and children you love." June dropped a dish. It shattered.

Her lip went out, her brows puckered as her resentment grew. "It's horrible to be a woman! Boys have all the freedom and fun."

She felt her mother's hand on her curls. "June, dear," her mother whispered, "some day, some year soon, you'll begin to learn how wonderful it is to be just what you are. It's not whether you are a boy or a girl, but how all the parts of you come together in one warm human being— and—" she gave a curl a light-hearted twist, "without us women there wouldn't be any boys!"

June tried not to hear, for she dreaded being cozy with her mother. When the dish towels were rinsed and hung in the sun, her mother said, "Go train your falcon, you'll learn a lot about birds . . . and yourself."

June carried the screaming sparrow hawk to the canoe landing, where the twins were making a hood for Ulysses. Their falconer's bag was opened. Leather and swivels, and leashes and knives decorated the landing.

Charles had already cut two thin strips of leather. Now, with head low and hands firm, he was putting three slits in them. Two at one end about an inch apart, the third at the far end.

"I like to make jesses," he said. "I think of the thirteenth century. And of Chaucer, and King Richard the Lion-hearted, and the people who lived when falconry flowered.

They used this same knot. It's that old, because it's so good. It will neither bind, nor slip off the bird's foot. Now hold him, June."

As she turned her bird over, his feet were in the air. This was the position in which he fought. He was surprised to be in it. But once there he had to fight, even against his will. His talons tensed, his feet shot out, his beak clamped onto June's thumb. She held on with a wince while Charles got the jesse around the foot. With a twist Zander bit so hard she let go. He flopped to the landing and backed up to take on all three giants.

June grabbed him and held him again. He fought harder. Finally he burst loose and flew over the landing toward the creek. But Don caught him under the breast just as the tips of wings and breast touched water. He held the dripping, screaming, angry bird, while Charles deftly jessed the other foot. He put the short end of the jesse around the leg and through the second hole, pulling until the first hole came out. Then he took the long end of the jesse and put it through the first hole. As he pulled, the strap tightened but did not bind, for the knot was perfect for its job.

Now holding the straps in his left fingers, Don placed his right hand under Zander's breast and pushed him up on his forefinger. The bird had one impulse when he felt the pressure of the jesses—to fly! With a plunge he was on his wings . . . and then he hung, head down, tripped by the jesses.

June gasped. Zander looked as if he were hurting himself. He "killied," the sparrow hawk distress cry. Then Don slipped his hand under his wet breast and righted the bird.

Zander flopped his head down again but this time twisted around and bit the boy.

"Man, he's got spunk!" Charles said with pleasure.

As he gathered Zander up for a third time, Don ran a swivel into the lower slits to hold the jesses to the leash. The swivel, which looked like a safety pin, had been bought at a fishing store. At the end of the leash the brothers tied a ring and put it over a pole. They put a round block of wood on the pole. And this ended the ritual of tethering the falcon.

"Now watch him!" Don said.

Zander stepped onto the soft leather-covered perch; he stood high, tail lifted. He drew himself up, pressed down his feathers and . . . flew. At the end of the leash he crashed to earth, then pulled and pulled and pulled. He screamed, "killie-killie." He fought.

The robins in the tree heard the devil cry of the bird of prey. They were nesting and they cried "cheet, cheet," their alarm cry of fear. The male robin boldly dove at Zander and struck him with a wing. But Zander, furious at his jesses, did not even notice. He flapped and pulled. The robins cried, the sparrow hawk fluttered and screamed.

June clenched her fists as the robin struck Zander, knocking him on his side. She started toward him.

"I must set him free so he can fight back," she cried.

Don and Charles laughed. "Oh, when the robins learn he's tied they'll stop hitting him. Just leave them alone to work out their problems." And the twins packed up their falconer's bag and ran to the house.

June waited until the screen door banged behind them.

Then she crouched low and, hands cupped, crept toward the terrified bird. She knew how to unsnap the swivel.

"I'm coming," she said. The robin screamed, raised its feathers in fright, then dove again at Zander. He struck June instead, a windy slap, and she fell toward her falcon. Zander, angry, terrified, turned on his back and slashed her hand with his talons. The pain was piercing. She drew into a ball and waited. Presently the robin stopped screaming and the falcon lay panting on his breast, wings spread. She picked him up and gently placed him on his perch. He shook, pecked his jesse, and fluffed in contentment.

June sat down on the sycamore roots and stared at her bird. He was sitting quietly, as if he could no longer feel the jesses.

A quiet hour later June wandered to the house to find her brothers. They were on the front porch talking to Uncle Paul and Will Bunker, a friend whose family had lived in the Cumberland valley for almost as long as the Pritchards. Will Bunker was a robust man. He laughed hard, and moved swiftly; he was full of energy and ideas. His face was round and impish, for Will Bunker was still part boy. The Pritchards all loved him dearly.

Obviously a complicated kind of male-play was afoot. Last year it had been a rattlesnake hunt in the mountains, with the dead snakes ending up in a box in her mother's living room marked "To Elizabeth, Flowers from the men-folks." When Mrs. Pritchard had said joyfully, "Oh, how lovely! Flowers for me!" and opened the box—they all had laughed, including Elizabeth. June, whenever she remembered her mother's laughter, was filled with admiration, and hoped that she would always be able to laugh at jokes played on her. Now, when teased, she could only cry or get angry.

As she listened to the men she wondered what would come of the game this year—laughter or tears. Will Bunker was saying, "And that cave is changing. Have you been in it this year, Paul?"

"No," her uncle answered. He ran his hand through his sparse blond hair and touched his toes together. He was easy and natural with children and adults. But boys were his joy, and to them he usually addressed his adventurous ideas, leaving June to needles and pots. He repeated, "No," then added, "but it's time to explore it again, I'm sure. I've loved that old cave ever since I was a boy."

"Well," said Will, "since the highway went over it, some of the boulders have sagged, and in one place they've dropped clean out of sight and opened a new passage. It goes down. I went in last week, and could see a huge new cavern with my flash. It looks like fun."

"Well, gee, let's go see it!" the twins said in one voice. "A new cavern in Bear Cave!"

Bear Cave was up the creek at the second bend. Once a year the Pritchard children, carrying picnic baskets, wedged themselves into it and explored its darkness. To June these were good, spooky adventures, for the old cave was cold and bat-filled and voices echoed back and forth. But the plans to go into a new and deeper room were leaving her out. And she wanted to go. She sat very close to Uncle Paul, hoping he would notice her. Nothing was said. She was a girl. Jim was not invited either. He was too young.

Rod was invited, because, as his father explained, "he's good on a rope." Wide-eyed, he accepted, though not because he loved Bear Cave—he didn't!—but because the big boys and tall men had invited him.

They departed that afternoon in the red canoe, with sandwiches, hot chocolate and root beer, a rope, flashlights and extra batteries. They took matches to test the air in the cave, and boots, in case of water.

June watched them go, standing on the creek bank holding her falcon on her fist. Don had just told her to "carry him until he stops fighting the jesses and leash," so she had picked him up as she walked toward the creek. The bird was comforting as she watched the canoe pull out, Will Bunker in the stern and Uncle Paul in the bow. The three boys sat on the bottom. As they swished off she lifted the leafy-smelling bird to her face, held his wings so he would not beat them, and whispered, "I'm good on a rope, too."

She jumped one-handed on the rope that swung out over the creek and looked up its length. Last year she had been able to climb to the top of the rope, much to her brothers' pride and pleasure. Now, she could only get halfway. Her arms weren't strong enough. Her legs and hips were too round. Growing up was filled with lonely changes.

The falcon on her wrist flapped in fright as he was carried out over the creek. The rope swung back over the land and June jumped off, holding Zander high. "You are tethered, pretty fellow, and so am I," she said to him. "I used to tag along behind when there were dangerous things to see. Now I'm not asked. I'm a girl, I must stay at home." Her soft whispering soothed him. Instead of sitting tense and skinny on her fist, Zander lifted his feathers. He was content.

June walked carefully to the edge of the landing, sat down and dangled her feet in the water. She whispered over and over to the bird on her wrist, "Please don't fight me. Please be happy, please, please."

Zander sat still. June touched her forehead against his warm beak—and as she did she smiled, for her world was now as peaceful as a summer day.

3. The Cave

When the men were not home at suppertime Elizabeth Pritchard was angry. When they did not appear at sundown she was worried. At dusk she was deeply concerned.

She called Mary Bunker on the phone and learned that Will had come home hours ago, dressed, and gone to a meeting. "That's odd," she said as she hung up. "Junie, let's get the green canoe and paddle up there. Maybe something's happened."

June's mother usually stayed out of the male world; the feminine arts were enough for her. But when her inner timing told her the male world was out of rhythm, she could paddle a canoe or shoot a gun or get angry. June knew when her mother's troubles were big—she lifted her chin and made decisions with determination.

She found a kerosene lamp, elaborately Victorian, which she filled and lit, for the men had taken the flashlights. Then June and her mother started up the creek as the shadows darkened in the willows and the lightning bugs stepped off the tips of grass blades to show their lights.

At the second bend they found the red canoe on the bank. They hopped out and pulled theirs beside. Her mother handed June the lamp, sat on a rock, and put the paddle across her knees. "All right, June," she said with firmness, "go in there and call. See if they're safe."

June felt her mother's courage pass on into her. She hesitated only long enough to say, "Oh, they're all right. This is silly."

"We'll see!" her mother said with finality. "Never whine when there's an important job to do. Whining's for children—and cats!"

June walked slowly toward the entrance of Bear Cave, staring at the black and gray limestones that framed the opening. She dropped to her knees. Bear Cave had to be entered on the stomach, wiggling through five feet of narrow stoneway. Her fear of the tight darkness seized her as she entered, but her mother's voice was so confident she pushed the lamp ahead of her and wedged in.

When she reached the big room beyond the passageway she stood up. The light from the lamp made eerie patterns over the vaulted walls. Water rushed somewhere in the dark. In a loud voice she called, "Hey, where are you?"

And ". . . *are you? . . . are you? . . . are you?*" answered back. The wind rushed out of the passageway. Stones dripped. Bats circled swift and quiet. June could feel her flesh go goose pimples. She stood still and called again.

From the darkness she heard, "June? Is that you? . . . *you? . . . you?*"

"Yes. Where are you? . . . *are you? . . . are you?*"

She watched her light create a leaping shadow on the wall and as it danced she opened her eyes wider to see the new cave-in Will Bunker had mentioned. It was black. And it rumbled with the sounds of a subterranean river carving holes in the belly of the earth. The sounds were cold and unfriendly. June fought down her urge to run. She walked to the passageway, wiggled into it, and called to her mother. "I hear them!"

"Thank heavens. Can you see them?"

"Not yet."

She dreaded going back to the cave-in; but she clenched her fists and backed up, walking slowly to the edge of the new opening. There she shouted into the earth.

"Are you all right? . . . *right? . . . right?*"

"No!" Uncle Paul answered. "We don't have lights. . . . *lights.* Rod fell off the rope. . . . *rope.* . . . collarbone, I think. . . . another rope. . . . flashlights . . . somewhere."

June held her kerosene lamp high and looked around. Cached by the big boulder where the rope was tied lay two flashlights.

"I found your lights," she called. She wondered why they were there.

"Good! Now, go . . . attic and get us that big rope. . . . *rope.*" It was Charles's voice. "Don't worry, we're okay. . . . *okay.* . . . *okay.*"

"Is Rod?"

"Yeah," Rod answered. "Snor toots (it hurts). . . . *toots.* . . . *toots.*" With Rod and the twins and Uncle Paul somewhere in its deep insides, the cave seemed a little more friendly. She looked around with confidence before she went to the entrance.

"I'll be back . . . *back.* . . . *back,*" she shouted. She wiggled between the great rocks, glad to be leaving the darkness, and reported to her mother.

"Honestly, you would think grown men like Paul and Will could take three boys into a cave without doing something stupid," her mother said, angry, now that her worries were relieved.

June shoved the canoe into the swift current. "Well, heck, they couldn't help it if the rope broke," she said. "Poor Rod," she added.

"You can bet that's not all of the story. With Will Bunker on an excursion, everything becomes more than adventure. It becomes high adventurous comedy. Mark my word." She paddled hard and straight, docked the canoe perfectly in the dark, and held to the landing while June ran up to the house and took two steps at a time to the attic.

She found the rope and returned to the canoe. When she handed the rope to her mother the weight sunk her arms. "Go get a ball of cord. You can't possibly climb down to them with this heavy thing. Throw them the cord ball, and tie the rope to it. Let them pull it down." June hurried back to the house for cord. She hummed as she picked it out of the table drawer, pleased to be part of the high adventure, at last.

They paddled back without talking. As the canoe was being beached a white shadow came softly overhead. It wheeled into a leaning willow. The shadow was Windy.

"No one fed him," June said, and laughed as she looked up to see the friendly old owl. He hissed, and they both felt reassured by his presence.

"He's not afraid of the dark," June said. "He loves it. I wish I did." But concern for Rod overcame her fear and she wiggled back into the cave on her stomach. It was easier this time, even with the bulky rope, for there were familiar voices inside.

As she crawled into the big room, a few bats swung low around the opening, waiting for her to unblock their exit. They dropped like stones and winged out the passage to hunt insects over the creek.

"I'm back," she called into the abyss.

"Okay! . . . *kay!* . . . *kay!*" answered the twins and the walls. "Now crawl down to that first ledge," came her uncle's voice. "Then call. I'll tell you . . . do next . . . *next.*" She hung a flashlight on her belt and looked down onto a broad ledge ten feet below. It was as dreary as the dark cellar—and as damp. She dropped the rope, stuck the ball of cord in her blouse, and clambered down to the ledge. There she stood, frightened to be going down into the earth. So she called to hear her own voice, "What do I do now?"

"Go to the right around the big stone. Climb down on

the next ledge. We are below that." The echoes were fewer.

She turned the light on the rocks and saw another great abyss. It vaulted like a huge dome above her head and plunged out of sight below. She could feel her head spin. Her knees stiffened and she could not step. Her feet would not lift even when she took a leg in both hands and pulled up on it.

She thought of Rod and the twins and Uncle Paul depending on her. She tried to summon courage. There was none to summon. She could only step back. So she did— two, three, four, and then she leaped against the wall and scrambled back to the entrance. "Mother!" she called, "Is Windy there?"

"Yes. Are you all right, June?"

"Yes, but I need Windy. Call him to you." She heard her mother whistle the Windy call. "Here he is!" Then June whistled. Carefully, curiously, skip-hopping as he looked and walked, the hungry owl came through the passage. June picked him up, fuzzy and warm, and kissed his soft neck.

"Come here," she said and walked to the first drop-off. The flashlight on her belt found foot camps. She climbed to the first landing and sat with her back pressed securely against the wall as she threaded the end of the cord ball into Windy's jesses. Then she set the old owl on a rock and unlooped about one hundred feet of string from the ball. Her feeling of elation was rising in triumph as she called out, "Whistle for Windy!" There was a long silence from below. Water rushed and splashed in some unlighted river.

Then Don cried, "Are you nuts? Get down here! . . . *here!* Rod's hurt. We need that rope. . . . *rope.* . . . *rope.*"

"Call him—please!" she screamed. There was another silence. Finally the Windy whistle bounced up among the rocks. The big owl stood in the darkness and shook. He listened, swung his head around in an enormous circle, and peered into the cave night.

June knew what his eyes were doing. Last summer she and Rod had played with him night after night with flashlights. In the dark the pupils of his eyes were so large they covered the iris as they took in the light that June and Rod would never know. When the lights went on the pupils became pinpoints so rapidly they could hardly see the owl eye adjust to the light. June knew that now Windy's eyes were taking in lights of far red and of night yellow as he saw rocks and crevasses and bats. The night had created his eyes.

"Keep calling!" June shouted. And the all-seeing Windy flew toward the whistle, down past the ledges to the men at the bottom. He chuttered hungrily when he reached them.

"Take off the cord and pull. The rope is tied to it."

At her side the rope began to unwind, and reel into the darkness of the abyss.

"We've got it!" three voices shouted. "Wrap it . . . boulder." June wrapped it and cried, "Okay."

"Is it firm?"

"I hope so."

"Hope so? It must be!" The rope went taut. There was a

long pause, then nimbly over the ledge below came her brother Charles, panting deeply. He crossed the next ledge and climbed up to June. "Hi," he said, and gave her a bear-hug. "Gee whizz! it's good to see you. That Will Bunker and his jokes. He had to go home early. We knew that. But just before he left we were jumping the boulders and he said 'Try it in the dark—I'll bet you can't.' Well, you know us—that's all we needed to hear. There was enough light from a hole up high and so, dopes that we were, we accepted the challenge. We gave Will our lights and ran over the big rocks . . . jumping, laughing, seeing as well as raccoons. Then we noticed Will was gone. We called and shouted . . . but he was off with all the lights!"

While Charles talked, he worked. "We got back to the ropes all right. We could see that well. And we would have had the last laugh, but when Rod started up the rope it frayed and broke. It had rubbed thin on a sharp stone as we came down. He fell only about seven feet; but we think he broke his collarbone. So there we were. We were sure glad to hear you 'cause Don and I were about to stand on each other's shoulders on top of Uncle Paul's to get one of us over the sheer drop. And there might have been two more busted collarbones."

As June held the flashlight he finished a mountain climber's sling out of the broken rope to put under Rod, tied a flashlight onto his belt, and disappeared over the ledge. With a few shouts and exclamations they hoisted Rod. They lifted him to the big room. June followed and sat down beside him.

"How are you?" she asked.

"Okay now," Rod said with a grin. "Let's go!"

When they were all out of the cave Rod curled up in the bottom of the canoe, and the expedition pushed off for home.

"Windy," Charles said. "Where's Windy?" There was a hiss in the willow and the owl swung down to his shoulder. Charles promised him a big fresh starling as soon as they reached home.

Their uncle took Rod to the doctor while Aunt Helen and June fixed fresh sheets on his cot. Then everyone waited for him in the warm kitchen, and they talked of the rope and Will and the lights. Finally Charles said to June in honest awe, "Whatever made you think of getting Windy?"

June was sitting on the table. She looked at her brother to say, "a stroke of genius." But the words would not come out. Instead she blurted, "I was too scared to move. I had to!" Fear was not a virtue in her brother's world, and she waited for the teasing she felt she deserved.

But Don surprised her, "That's all right. It was a *great* idea. It's good to be afraid if it makes you think . . . and you sure did!"

"Well, Windy made me think, too. I see what you mean by a well-trained bird. I'll work harder with Zander."

The twins grinned at her in pleasure. She was a heroine in her brothers' eyes. And it was pleasant—just awfully pleasant and rewarding.

4. Trained

Will Bunker was at the house before dawn, knocking at the doors and windows. Charles crawled down the rainspout and greeted him with the news about Rod. Will, who had known and loved Rod since he was a baby, cried out loud in his shame. He threw open the door and rushed up to the sleeping porch. He tiptoed gently to the far cot and dropped to his knees to put his arms around the sleeping boy.

"Forgive me, Rod. I didn't want it to work out this way. I came back to the cave after my meeting and I couldn't find you all. I was sure all you nimble and wonderful

Pritchards had climbed out. I know you boys climb cliffs, jump over boulders in streams, swing up trees—you can do anything out of doors; and I guess I didn't think. I just didn't think anything could happen to any of you." He paused.

Rod opened his eyes and smiled. "Aw, it doesn't hurt anymore." He sat up to prove it.

"You're a hero," said Will.

"No, Windy is the hero." And he told Will about the owl.

When Will came down to the kitchen, Elizabeth Pritchard was up and about. She was furious with him. She scolded the child in him. And he took a long, deep breath and answered her like a man.

"Sometimes I don't understand boys, Elizabeth. I guess it's because I have only girls. I think boys can do everything a man can do, but with more spirit. I guess they really *are* young—their bones and their brains." He sat down and rubbed his hands in his hair. June overheard him as she stepped into the kitchen. Shyly, she walked over to him and touched his shoulder.

"Will, I'm going to train Zander so that he can be as wonderful as Windy." Then she sighed, "And that means work."

She went to get the lure, tied a bit of beef on it, and ran out to the maple tree. Will and her mother were forgotten as she whistled and held up the birdlike lure, a block of wood, decorated with feathers. She called and waited . . . called and waited . . . called and waited until the sun was hot and her new resolve to call Zander to her fist growing weak. Three hours later, he was hungry enough to fly to her. "Pheew!" she said, and was glad she had stayed with her job.

For ten days June got up at dawn and called Zander to her fist. And it was work, boring work. She stood and called, and waited again and again, and called, each day. Zander seemed to prefer starvation to bending to her will. As the days passed she grew bored, and wondered each morning whether her father was right. Would she have the stick-to-itiveness to master the bird?

But on the eleventh day Zander flew to her in half the time. She petted him and talked to him. He tilted his head the better to let her voice fall on the flat drum of an ear that lay under his feathers.

On Friday afternoon her father came for the weekend. During the summer he commuted only on weekends from his job as an entomologist for the government. June watched the road for him. As he drove into the yard, she met him with a leaping hug. "Zander will fly to me from the maple tree to the middle of the yard," she said as she hung on his neck.

Charles Pritchard, Sr., looked at his undisciplined daughter. "That's a start. But you're not nearly there. Work harder!"

"But that's good!"

"It's good, but not excellent!" It was in moments like these that she wanted to fight her father. She stomped to the maple and lifted the buffy-breasted falcon upon her finger. His beautiful flat head tilted as he looked at her. Deftly she untied the leash from the pole and walked down the yard with him. She crossed the railroad tracks and pushed through the joe-pye weeds to the meadows.

"It's no use," she said to Zander. "I thought I was doing a good job. . . . I might as well give you up . . . oh phooey."

In anger she unsnapped the swivel in the jesses and twisted it out of the leather holes. The bird sat free on her hand.

"I never do anything well enough," she cried, and felt so sorry for herself she threw the bird into the air. "Go away. Go away."

Immediately she regretted her action. Zander danced on his wings and whirled over her head. He circled, and took to the sky. She called, furious with herself for "cutting off her nose to spite her face." She knew she was hurting only herself and she did not like it.

There was no food with which to lure the bird back. June could only whistle and swing her arm. Zander climbed higher: above the willows, over the sycamore, up to the tall ash, and into the hot white sky.

She watched him bank and tip onto a high river of wind and ride it like a bullet beyond the swimming hole. She whistled. And then climbed the fence to balance herself on the rail.

"Come down here, Zander!" she pleaded. She could feel the tears running warm down her cheeks. "Please come," and she lifted her hand. Suddenly—and she did not even see it happen—her hand was struck; she toppled, she jumped, and Zander fluttered above her. She held out her arm again and her falcon settled upon it as beautifully as a ballerina. In relief, June wept openly and hard.

"That was wonderful . . . not just good . . . but marvelous. Ulysses couldn't do better." June talked on and on as she slipped her thumb and forefinger around the jesses, held Zander tight, then looked for an insect for a reward. The meadow grasses bounced with grasshoppers; and she finally caught one and fed it to the falcon. While he ate she promised herself that she would never again turn him loose in spite. The loneliness had been too deep.

As she crossed the railroad tracks to go home, she stopped on the hot cinders to study him, wondering what she had done to reach his small bird brain and make him react. She knew they could not communicate, except through whistles and screams . . . and yet the bird had known what she had wanted, and he had come to her.

Suddenly she became aware that words were not the only way to express ideas, and she whispered, "Now you and I have a secret language, too." She skipped home.

June did not tell anyone of Zander's flight. She was afraid they would ask to see the falcon fly free. And she feared that the next time Zander would not come back. But for the following week she trained the bird with the first real interest she had ever had in everyday routine. She knew now what training could do.

The new training period went on for about two weeks . . . and then . . . her mother took her to town on market day. Elizabeth Pritchard went every Saturday morning to buy vegetables and fruits and chickens and eggs in the farmers' market.

The market was on the square, an old red brick building with stalls around the outside and an enormous three-story cathedral-like room inside. As soon as she stepped inside,

June always bent back to see the vaulting beams and girders and the sparrows high in the eaves. They amused her in their private world at the top of the market, talking and fluttering and scrapping, above the din of the buyers and sellers below.

The Brethren and the Amish of the countryside brought in their foods every week to sell, and their counters were mounds of color. The women in their gray dresses and bonnets offset the red apples and yellow squash. The purple eggplants blended with the black hats and pants of their men.

June's mother went very early Saturday to get the best buys. She delighted in visiting many stalls before she made up her mind which jewel of a pepper or apple to buy. This day she cut down her pleasure. She shopped quickly, then parked her baskets under Mr. Breneman's stand and led her daughter across the street to the town department store. Her brown heels clicked hard on the brick walk and her movements were fast and deliberate. June sensed a growing-up crisis. She hung back, trying to avoid another frictiony burst as her mother tried to shape her for adulthood.

They turned into the plain brown store. They passed the stony clerks at the button counter and marched on toward the back of the store and behind the stacks of yard goods. This was the underwear department. The plan was clear even before her mother said with a warm and nice smile, "It's time to buy you a brassiere and a little light girdle." June wanted to disapppear.

A saleslady smiled and her smile was too sweet.

"Mother," June murmured in pain, "please, can't we

wait?" She grew angry at the saleslady, as well as her mother. As she turned to flee she saw the grinning, thin, store owner, Mr. Shide. He, too, knew; and June hated him all over, even to the laces in his shoes on which her eyes fastened in humility.

There was nothing to do but stand through the embarrassing ordeal, the measurements, the smiles, the pleasantries, the fitting . . . and finally, the acceptance of the green paper bag at arm's length like a leaky bucket. As the saleslady said good-bye June seemed to see millions of shining teeth standing around her words, "You'll look sweet, dearie." June wanted to bite . . . even the counter.

Somehow she got home. She carried the paper bag to her room, three steps at a time, opened the bottom bureau drawer and stuffed it in. She stomped out of the room to the head of the steps. She listened. The car was being unloaded of its bountiful baskets, the boys were carrying in bundles, Rod was trying to play his flute in spite of his broken collarbone. She turned in the confusion, flew back to the drawer, opened it, and peeked in the bag. Carefully she lifted out the garments and stared at them. There they were, very real, representing a whole long, unwritten life that lay ahead, mysterious and exciting. She wondered about marriage and childbearing and nursing and buckets and brooms. Then she put the garments back in the bag. She closed the drawer.

All down the dark back stairs the young lady walked with a swing of her hips, with a toss of her head. At the bottom she opened a door and saw Charles. She didn't want him to see her flounce, so she jumped down the last step. He gave her a quick, friendly punch; she sparred with him. He touched her shoulder; she socked back, stumbled, missed— and went sprawling into the dining room.

"You're a puppy!" Charles teased.

June thought of the package in the drawer upstairs and answered with a toss of her head, "That's what you think!" Charles's face puzzled, his eyes studied the mystery of his sister.

"Don't be that kind of a girl," he said. "Don't play silly secret games."

June knew what he meant. She was being flashy and it did not go with the upbringing he and Don had given her. They thought she should be honest and open and natural about all things, from climbing a rope to becoming a woman. June was abashed. She punched him hard and ran out the back door to the maple tree and her falcon.

Zander stepped to her finger the moment it was offered. She dug her nose in his feathers and said to the bird, "At times it's very hard to know who I really am." And the tears stood along the rims of her eyes.

For the rest of the day June had no interest in working with her falcon. She just held him on her fist.

Don was working with Ulysses, the tiercel. Ulysses had broken a tail feather and Don was "imping" a new one in for him. It was not a duck hawk tail feather, but a Cooper's hawk, one Jess had moulted. A broken feather made flying difficult for Ulysses. He lost speed, so Don was carefully cutting and, with some airplane dope and wire, imping the new feather into the broken base of the old. June carried Zander to his side and watched.

"It's not as pretty as his own feather," she said.

"No, and it's a little long. But it'll work. He'll hunt better. You'd better watch that ring at the base of Zander's perch, or he'll be breaking feathers, too. He was banging yesterday."

Presently the back door opened and Charles senior and Uncle Paul strode down the yard with hammers, saw, and nails to fix the canoe landing.

They stood chest-deep in the creek, hammering and arguing about where the new supporters should be nailed. Uncle Paul finally changed the subject. "Will Bunker came by the office today. Left a nice book for Rod." June listened in a half-world. Uncle Paul continued. "He's about to close a big deal on his textile mills. Double their output and profits. A man has come in from California to invest in his business."

There was a long pause as the two men worked as a team.

"Will said he and Mary are giving a big party Monday night for the man. . . . All business people from the plant. They hired Ross Mort to play music, bought seven turkeys, five hams . . . and are getting a woman from Philadelphia to help decorate. . . . It's going to be a humdinger. . . ."

June was listening completely now. The Bunkers were splendid when they did things. And this party sounded of castle grandeur; it glittered in the top of her mind.

A few nights later at dinner, they were all seated around the table in the old converted parlor. The tablecloth was red, the wallpaper plaid. It was gay to everyone but Charles senior. The room still reminded him of piano lessons and funerals, the only events for which the parlor was used when he was a boy.

On the table was a casserole of chicken pot pie covered with homemade biscuits. There were stewed tomatoes, cold sliced cucumbers, breaded eggplant, cranberry sauce, and blueberry pie. Elizabeth Pritchard was a marvelous cook even on her shaky kerosene stove. In contrast, Aunt Helen was no cook at all. She disliked the entire process; and so, that night, on the other side of the house the Paul Pritchards were having a kind of white stew and potato salad. Suddenly Uncle Paul tiptoed through the door, spying on the food. "Wow!" he said and picked up a plate.

The young people chuckled, for Uncle Paul always checked the tables in the house to see which had the best food, and when he found a special delicacy he snitched some. He was usually gracious and he admired all the food everywhere with ecstatic words; but Elizabeth Pritchard's he ate.

He was sneaking back with chicken pot pie and cranberries when they heard him roar out a laugh. He reappeared in the doorway.

"Look!" he said. In the center of his plate sat Bobu, the screech owl. "He thought the cranberry sauce was his dinner!" Uncle Paul held the plate high so they could see the little gray owl sitting straight and surprised in the red sauce.

June stared at Bobu on the plate, and suddenly it was no longer Uncle Paul holding him there, but Will Bunker, and he was in a dinner jacket and was embarrassed before his distinguished guest.

"I wish Bobu would sit on Will Bunker's plate next Monday," she said.

Uncle Paul looked at her. His eyes twinkled, his face

broke into a thousand glad crow's feet, and he came toward her slowly. "What an idea, what a wonderful, marvelous idea." He put down his plate and picked up Bobu in his hand. Turning the bird over he wiped the funny feet that go two toes and two toes when sitting and spread out in the four directions of the compass when closing on prey. He released the owl and Bobu flew to the victrola to wait for someone to wind it up and mend his disappointed heart.

Uncle Paul gave the victrola a flip, and sat down. "Listen," he said with enthusiasm, "we'll get our whole menagerie over to the Bunkers' party . . . and boy! will that be a surprised guest of honor! The orchestra leader will help. Will Bunker pulled a practical joke on him once. He'll be delighted to get even."

For the next week everyone at Pritchard's planned and plotted and invented marvelous things to do at the Bunker party.

Monday night arrived. Uncle Paul drove the surprise party in his car and parked in the cornfield behind the Bunker house. Then the Pritchards, both wild and tame, stole quietly along the country road. June carried Zander. Don led the family dogs, Spike and Brownie. Rod had Windy, Jim walked with Bobu and Fingers, and Charles and Uncle Paul carried buckets of minnows and catfish.

They came in the back way behind the high hedge. June peeked through the dense leaves to see on the lawn a white table around which sat the guests, all glittering, all beautiful. Above their heads hung brightly colored Japanese lanterns; crystal shone, china belled at the touch of silverware. She was transfixed.

Don said, "Come on, Junie, they'll see you," and she followed the group through the big French doors off the dining room into the open, shining living room where Ross, the orchestra leader, was waiting.

There she spun in joy. The room was decorated in white; white flowers, candles, paper lanterns, white chairs to sit upon. In a spell of wonder she sat Zander, as planned, on the marble boy on the mantel.

But Zander was beautiful and he gave dignity to the little bare boy—not humor. June was surprised and glad. Her falcon could not be changed by silly pranks. He rose above them.

The glamour did not bother the men and boys. Charles and Uncle Paul were laughing as they carried the buckets of fish toward the ladies' powder room.

Charles put three bewhiskered catfish into the washbowl. Uncle Paul poured minnows into the clear, roiling water of the old bathtub. His grin was enormous.

Rod, by the old victrola, was whispering excitedly to Ross. "Please open it after they all get dancing and wind it up a little bit." Then, lizard-like, he climbed the bookcase and placed Bobu quietly in a space between the books. Bobu settled in as if it were a hollow tree. Bobu was well fed, and he fluffed his feathers, pulled up a foot, and squinted down upon the band.

Uncle Paul next took a bag of aniseed out of his pocket and tied a string to it. He dragged it across the dance floor, out the back French doors, around the house, into the front doors, and across the floor to complete an enormous circle. Aniseed is used to make trails to train hunting dogs. Brownie and Spike loved to follow the odor over the house at Pritchard's, howling and barking. Now they would go through their routine in the Bunker house.

The last arrangement was made as Charles quickly taught the clarinetist Windy's whistle. Then the Pritchards crossed the porch and dropped into the bushes to wait and watch. Fingers, the raccoon, was still in a box. He could be released when the punch and cookies were served.

It wasn't long before Will Bunker stepped through the patio door into the dining room. He was talking seriously to a heavily built man, with a black moustache, several chins, barrel-chest, and enormous cigar. This must be Mr. Sparter, the guest of honor.

Will walked through the dining room across the hall and stepped into the living room. Mort lifted his baton and started the music.

This frightened Zander. He killied. Will turned, Mr. Sparter turned. They looked. They shrugged, they laughed, and then Mr. Sparter, who was behind Will, facing the mantel, stared over Will's curly hair. He bit his cigar, rocked on his toes, and stared harder. He cleared his throat.

Will sensed his guest's confusion, thought he'd said something wrong, tried to smooth his error—then turned to see Zander. Other guests were coming in: young men, old men, and women in beautiful gowns. The music soared. Then Ross walked across the room, opened the victrola, and said to Will, "We have some amusing old records for intermission." He wound the machine and turned it on. Bobu stepped forward in his niche. He bobbed his head up, down, then around and around as his yellow and black eyes focused on the "Bobu Amusement Park." He jumped on his wings and flew softly over heads, alighting on the turntable. There were polite gasps from the women. Bobu became alarmed, took off, and winged around the room. Cries mounted, voices sounded in alarm until he finally found a door and wheeled into the darkness. From the bushes, Rod called him down.

The clarinetist arose and, tipping back his head, whistled the Windy call. The old fellow on Jim's fist bobbed his head and flew. He went in the open French door and circled the room. Finally he settled on the back of Mrs. Sparter's chair. She screamed and before the other guests reached her, Uncle Paul released Spike and Brownie, gave them the scent of the aniseed, and whispered, "Go git it!"

Through the French doors ran Spike, head low, yiping along the trail, passing beaded skirts, going between black broadcloth legs, straight out the far French doors, around the house and back in the front doors again. He was followed by big lumbering Brownie. Will was stony white. He recognized the dogs. He shouted and swished them out, then closed the door after them. But they circled the house and came in the front door again, noses to the ground, Spike yiping, Brownie woofing in his bullfrog basso. They ran to the rear doors, found them closed, jumped on them, pushed them open, and bellowed out into the night again. They circled the house. Now Will threw himself against the front windows and would not let the barking dogs in.

Charles, standing in the bushes, was laughing so hard he buckled over to hold his aching sides.

The "palace" was bedlam. Then Jim slipped into the

dining room and placed Fingers on the table. He petted him and showed him the cookies. Fingers wasn't discovered until a few minutes later when the laughing Mr. Sparter came into the dining room for a drink of punch. He stopped and threw his hands in the air when he saw the raccoon, all four feet in the beverage, chasing the ice cubes.

Will Bunker, tie undone, smudged with dirt, clutched Mr. Sparter's arm. "Please, excuse this fiasco. This is an outrage. I know who's done this. Please excuse me, they must be around. I am so sorry. This is unforgivable."

Uncle Paul liked that. He laughed from his belly.

"Who are they?" Mr. Sparter roared happily and followed Will to the porch.

"Paul!" Will shouted. "Where are you? Come on! Stop! Please stop! I'm sorry about the cave. I apologize again. But this is too much. Paul!"

Uncle Paul, arms swinging freely, moving as naturally as wind, went up onto the porch. June ran around him and dashed for Zander.

As the other birds and animals were gathered, Mr. Sparter followed the children, laughing and shaking his head.

"This is hysterical," he said, stroking old Windy. "Do you children train all these birds and beasts?" Charles nodded. "Do the falcons hunt as they did in the days of Chaucer?"

"We hope so."

The other guests gathered around in delight. Then Uncle Paul with his most charming smile called, "Good-night," and herded his group off the porch. As they packed them-selves into the car Uncle Paul said, "My only regret is that

I will not hear the women when they discover the fish." The twins laughed, Rod laughed. But June thought of the music and the fish and for a moment she was sad that so lovely a ball had been spoiled.

Charles was laughing softly to himself, then louder and louder until he said through his chuckles, "And Spike and Brownie going, noses down, around and around . . ."

Uncle Paul roared, and Don and Jim and Rod. June tried to remember the beauty, the flowers, the lights . . . but soon she too giggled, chuckled, and finally rolled against the side of the car and laughed with the rest.

At dawn the boys on the sleeping porch were awakened by a fire cracker being thrown in their midst. They all leaned over the railing to see Will Bunker in his dinner jacket shouting, "All you Pritchards get up! Time to feed the owls, time to feed the hawks. Get up! Everybody get up!"

Uncle Paul came down in his pajamas and tried to hush him, but he could not. Will continued to shout. "I was mad as Billy-be-darned last night; then I found you made my party a success. A great success. Al Sparter was so amused by the hawks and owls and dogs and children that he offered me enough money to double the plants . . . wants to take everyone to dinner, especially Windy.

"Al's a big-thinking man, alive and fun and no nonsense. We're going to go to Africa together . . . to fish and swim."

The twins climbed down the porch posts, Rod blundered sleepily down the back steps. Jim hung over the railing, as the bright word "Africa" sparked everyone's imagination.

5. *The Solo*

Each day there was dawn. The orange sun would stand behind the barn—and it was time to fly Zander. June had set this as her hour to work and followed it well for fourteen days, but the schedule was hard to maintain. On the fifteenth day she said to the sun, "In a minute, in a minute." She felt the cool sheets, the soft pillow . . . and snuggled deep in the old brass bed.

Hours later her mother called her to breakfast. As she dressed June promised herself she would fly Zander when the dishes were washed and dried.

Don and Charles, coming back from the barn with the

day's supply of falcon food, called to their sleepy sister on
the stairs, "Did you exercise Zander?"

"No, I'll do it after breakfast."

"I betcha don't," Charles said.

"Not right after breakfast!" her mother said. "This is
laundry day, and I need you."

As the last dish was being put away, the front door banged
and the dogs barked and Fingers, the raccoon, came running
around the porch to climb the maple and hide. The falcons
flattened their feathers and watched him in some alarm.
Fingers often teased the birds, but never harmed them, for
an inner sense and a bad experience with Ulysses told him
of the might of the falcon. The birds, however, were never
relaxed when Fingers came to the maple. But Spike and
Brownie could move between them without flattening a
single feather in anxiety.

Then all the birds and the raccoon stared at the porch
. . . they heard Will Bunker before he turned the corner
calling, "Anyone at home?" Laughing and happy he strode
into the kitchen where he was greeted by the family. He
flipped a chair around and sat in it backwards.

After he had inquired about Rod, who still troubled his
conscience, he announced with a rock of the rockerless
chair, "I've stopped by to say good-bye! Tomorrow we're
off for Africa!"

Elizabeth Pritchard turned on him in astonishment. "So
soon?"

He nodded. "Al Sparter and I want to see the whale
migration off the coast and fish a bit. Mary and Mrs. Sparter

will stay here." There was a hiss at the door. Hungry Windy was on the back of a porch chair, calling to get in.

"Why are you awake?" Charles called to the owl as he opened the door. Windy flew in and perched on the kitchen mantel.

"That's a great owl," Will said.

Elizabeth nodded and added, "He's been acting strange lately, wilder, more distant. I think the twins ought to tie him up awhile."

Will looked at sleepy June, "And how is your falcon, little cave climber?" She smiled. Suddenly he said, "Hey, what about a falcon hunt when Mr. Sparter and I get back? Your Zander," and he turned to the twins, "your Ulysses, Jess, Screamer, Bobu, Windy, the whole gorgeous affair. All these falcons, and I've never seen one do anything but go up and down the yard on a leash."

"Well, sure," both twins said at once. "About the end of August when the weather's not so heavy. When will you be back?"

"The twenty-sixth—we aren't staying long."

"How about the twenty-eighth?"

Will Bunker said "Fine. Fine!" and rocked back and forth on the chair.

Charles nudged June. "You'd better train your bird."

But her mother said, "June, get the tubs out and put them in the yard. The water's boiling, and I don't want this laundry to drag on all day."

And all day June was "too busy," and did not fly her falcon.

When dawn came the next day she remembered too well the sweet joy of yesterday's sleep. She did not awake early the next, nor the next, nor the next. And the twins were right. If the birds weren't flown before breakfast, life in the Pritchard house became too full to stop.

And then there was Emily Barnes. Emily lived up the road in the old stone house, and although she had been there for years, June barely knew her . . .

Until the day she came running down the road, head back, eyes crinkled and lit with highlights, to tell June that a band of gypsies had camped in the meadow overnight. At dawn the gypsies had stopped at Mrs. Bunkelbarger's house and forced her to give them all her egg money—seven dollars. Then they took a drink from her pump and drove away. Emily said, "I must go see where they have been." And June untied her apron to follow her, for poor, starving gypsies, unloved, unwanted, were June's idea of the most romantic people in the world. She often dreamed that a band would come to her yard at night and carry her away to sing and dance in the fields and meadows. She smoothed her springy curls with her palms, thrilled to hear that gypsies had been near, and ran out the back door with Emily.

"You'd better fly Zander," the twins called.

And June called back, "In a minute, in a minute."

The dust puffed under the four running bare feet, and the minute became four hours.

On Friday night her father came up from the city. She did not run to meet him, for his first question was always, "Well, how's the training coming?" And what could she say? Almost ten days had passed and she had merely thrown sparrows to the falcon as she and Emily ran off to the meadow to talk under the jimpson weeds about the beautiful world of romance.

To avoid her father June threw a piece of meat to Zander (sometimes when wild food ran out the falcons and owls were fed beef chunks or chicken necks). Then she ran to the creek to swim with Emily. At dinner it was apparent to Charles senior that his daughter had not done much falcon training. He said, "It really doesn't matter, I guess, except that you'll lose your bird if you don't train him. Unless, of course, you just want a tethered bird on a perch—which is different from a bird on wing with spirit." He paused and added, "But as long as you feed him and are gentle to him, I guess I can't complain."

June was annoyed. Her father was telling her again to see a project through to the end. She felt incapable and irritated. She wanted to get angry with him, but did not know how.

After dinner all the Pritchards gathered by the canoe landing to sing and talk. In the middle of a song her father said, "Look at Windy."

The old owl was sitting on the back of the rocking chair on the porch and was swinging his head in enormous circles. His eyes were focused on the sky beyond the barn. There seemed to be an urgency about him.

"You'd better leash him, Charles," Elizabeth said to her son. Quickly he moved forward to take the bird's jesses; but it was too late. The old owl, his eyes on something far beyond human sight, dropped to the ground, ran with wings lifted and took off. He flew east. He alighted in the white pine at the edge of the yard. June watched her brother follow the bird to the tree and start to climb.

Everyone whistled and called, for obviously something was happening to Windy. He seemed neither to hear nor to remember. No one could get to his brain. And then, still not looking back, still seeing only the sky, he took off for the roof of the house just as Charles reached out for him. There he ran across the peak and lifted himself softly to the chimney.

Don ran up the porch post, like a native up a palm, rolled onto the roof and jumped against the wall of the house. His fingers in the whirligigs, toes in the decorative wooden flowers, he clambered up the side of the house to the top of the sleeping porch. Then bouncing, flying, he leaped across the porch roof to the slate peak of the house, and balancing with his arms out, lightly ran to the chimney.

A few feet away from the owl he stopped and held out his hand. "Windy," he called; then softly, "Windy look at me. Come on."

The owl circled his head, swung it low like a pendulum over his feather-fuzzy feet and kept his eye on the sky. Even Don's hand did not distract him. Often the owls would fix on a stir of the curtains, the twirl of a light cord; even meat stuck in front of their eyes would not be seen, so single-minded are they. But a whistle, a sound, usually would get to them. Now, nothing seemed to penetrate the small brain of the beloved barn owl.

Far down in the yard below the Pritchards watched breathlessly. Each remembered the cave and the owl's warm obedience. But all this had suddenly disappeared. Windy was a stranger.

"He's wild again," said Elizabeth Pritchard. "It's as if he were another bird." And with that, as Don swung upon the jesses, the owl lifted himself onto his milky-tan wings, and, beating them silently and deeply, flew over the white pine, the railroad, the store, past the hill farm to his speck in the sky.

And each knew he would never see Windy again.

Rod ran to the edge of the yard, holding his hand high, saying nothing. Aunt Helen looked up, her brown eyes glistening wet. June dropped her head.

Under the quilt that night she lay wide awake, feeling the stitches on each patch, the ribbon that circled the edge. She felt these things to stay open-eyed, for when she closed her eyes she saw Zander at the Falconry Meet watching the sky . . . to fly to Windy. And no whistle, no call, no food would bring him back.

She must arrange to avoid the Meet.

The stars were still big when she got up the next morning. She went down the back steps to the kitchen, found a sparrow wrapped in paper in the left-hand side of her mother's icebox, and sat outside on the porch until Zander could see in the dawn. Then she flew him ten times to her hand, giving him a nibble each time to reward his effort.

The following morning at dawn June worked Zander again. Half an hour later the twins came down to exercise Ulysses and Comet, the Cooper's hawk. The other Cooper's, Screamer, was not training well. As Charles picked her up he said, "You know, I might as well let Screamer go. She's a sluggish, lazy bird . . . and stupid. She's really not worth the time I'm putting in on her.

"It's funny," he went on, "how different birds can be. They're like people; each has his own personality and characteristics and there isn't much anyone can do about them. Now, there sits Comet—lively, fast, energetic—out of the same nest as Screamer. And I'll bet Comet will be a sensation at the Meet, and Screamer will go up in a tree and won't remember which is hand and which is air . . . she's so dumb."

Screamer picked up a foot and scratched her head with a toe. Charles whistled her three notes and she did not budge. He whistled it again and she scratched her shoulder.

"She's starved," he said, "yet she forgets that this whistle means food. I have to *show* her the food, then I have to whistle until finally the rubbery old wheels grind in that small head and she says to herself, 'Oh, food!' just so surprised as if it had never happened before."

He showed Screamer the food. She packed her feathers down to her body with interest and then scratched again. Charles stepped back and whistled. She cocked her pretty head, remembered the food she had seen, and flew to the gauntlet on Charles's hand. She ate and came to him twice again. Not fast, not brightly, but methodically.

June watched—and was grateful for Zander.

On the twenty-third of August, Don and Charles announced "Z" day. "We'll fly Zander free. You've worked him hard and well. He's ready."

"NO!" June cried. "No, he'll leave. Let's wait—wait until the Falconry Meet."

"And have all the people scare him to death and start him off for the mountains . . . uh uh. He'll be all right, honest. You've done a better job than you think."

She was sent to the icebox for sparrows. When she came out the boys were trooping off to the field, and Comet was sitting erect on the gauntlet on Charles's hand.

"Bring Zander!" Don shouted.

"No!" June called.

"Yes, you must!"

Reluctantly she lifted her falcon from the perch and carried him to the field. "Zander first," the twins declared.

Don stood at the edge of the yellow stubbled wheat field, June walked into the middle. She held the lure in her hand. Zander sat unleashed on Don's finger. He gently held the jesses.

Don called, "Ready?"

He was answered, "Yes!"

He threw Zander up on the air to get the falcon airborne. June held the lure and whistled. Zander sped down the field, low over the bright stubble, coming toward her with precision and beauty.

"Hold your hand up!" Don shouted. She did. Zander snatched the meat on the lure, it came off, and he winged up . . . up into the sky, carrying the food on over the field to the apple orchard beyond . . . and out of sight.

"No, no," June cried, and ran hard. She was desperate.

Jim, Rod, Don ran. Charles took Comet back to the yard and followed on his toes. They jumped the fence and raced into the gray twisted trees of the orchard. They all whistled. There was no answer. They peered up into the branches, walked, called. There was no reply.

"Well," said Don, "we'll have to give up and try again tomorrow. He'll eat the food and be too stuffed to come back. When he's hungry again we can call him in. He's around here, but quiet and full."

The twins knew the quest was useless. They departed.

But June would not give up. She was sure he would get his jesses caught on a limb and die.

She sat alone in the orchard and listened to the wind splash in the leaves and the insects beat out a dull chorus, out of rhythm with the wind. It was hot. Voices from the stream made her lonely. With her head on her knees she let the tears roll. She wanted the bird desperately. She needed his bright silent companionship. She needed to love something that was safe and sure.

She did not go home for dinner. The twins came out to get her, but she did not move. Later they came back with a sandwich and word from her mother that she had better come home—or else.

Don said with gentle warmth, "He was always a strong-minded little bird, but that's why you like him . . . and so nice. He'll be back."

June had no answer. And Don left her there.

Miserable and tired she walked among the trees calling and whistling. Finally it was night. The bird would not move in the dark. He was safe until dawn.

She climbed the fence to go home—and suddenly heard

near the edge of the orchard the soft chittering of a contented sparrow hawk. She stepped down, saw a movement, and spotted Zander.

She knew she should wait but she couldn't. She jumped into the tree and climbed up the gray limbs. Her sudden too-swift movements frightened the bird, and he flew into the darkness.

"Oh, come back! Come back!" she called, and leaned far out, reaching into the shadows. But to flush a falcon in the dark might be fatal. He would blunder into an unprotected place. She climbed down and ran home.

"Don! Charles!" she called. "I scared Zander into the night."

The twins dropped their books and arose. They frowned alike, a double concern. Flopping around after sundown would make the little falcon available to the big barred owls of the area. If he touched the ground the foxes and weasels would get him. Don and Charles had lost other hawks this way. They wanted to be helpful, but could only say, "Well, there's nothing to do now. Go to bed. We'll get up before the sun."

June crawled into the brass bed and lay face-down on the pillow. There came a knock at the door. "Le fours jay?"

"Come in, Rod," she answered in English.

He poked his head in the door and said, "We'll start another Clayforbia."

"O, spid! (a curse word)" June cried, and pushed her face deeper into the pillow.

An hour passed and there was another rap on the door.

"Come in."

"In fact, you can be the mayor this year," Rod said sweetly.

But June did not even smile. "I don't want anything but the morning to come."

She waited all night for the stars to move across the sky. When Orion showed in the left-hand corner of her window she got up. It was still dark. Fingers, the raccoon, came out from the corner of the sleeping porch, pushed open the screen door and started down the steps behind her. She picked him up and carried him back upstairs to his barrel. Bobu was sitting on the porch railing, bobbing and swinging his head as he looked over the dawning world. All the boys were asleep. The dogs were, too.

Then Jim, sensing movement around him, awakened. He whistled to Bobu, who jumped, flapped, and ran to him. Jim saw June. He sat up.

"What do you want, Junie?"

"I'm going to the apple orchard. Hold Fingers, he'll follow me." Jim stepped out of bed and took the raccoon. Fingers stuck his hands in Jim's pocket and mouth, feeling, feeling, with his incessant hands, for shapes and textures and something to stuff in his jaws.

Jim threw his head back, looked into the yard and said, "Junie, I think I see Zander."

"No!" she said. "No, you don't! Don't fool me."

"Well, there's something sitting on his perch and it looks like him." Jim's voice was sincere, breathless.

She ran to the railing and leaned far out.

In the blue-green light of predawn she saw her falcon.

Her mother had told her often that at thirteen it was unladylike to climb down the rainspouts and posts, but she was over the railing and down on the grass before she remembered. She ran to the perch. Zander, handsome with his brick-red cap and black eyes, chuttered and jumped to her hand. He was glad to see her. She put her fingers over the jesses, held tight, and slipped on the leash. Then she called, called to everyone.

"Zander is back! He's back and on his perch!" and the house stirred and relatives came to windows or ran down steps to see the returned bird.

"He'll be all right now," Don said. "He's your bird. You've trained him enough to fly him in the hunt."

"Have I? Have I?" She felt the mystery of having done a job. It was a strange, round feeling—and she liked it.

Three hours later while she and her mother were rinsing dishes, the telephone rang. Uncle Paul, dish towel tied around his waist as he washed pots for Aunt Helen, answered it.

He said nothing but hello, then stood and listened. The towel slowly unwound and fell to the floor. Rod and Jim were playing checkers and they stopped moving men to stare at their father. They knew something terrible had happened.

Uncle Paul hung up the 'phone and addressing none and all, said slowly, "Will Bunker is dead. He drowned yesterday off the coast of Africa . . . an undertow took him."

Rod cried, "Oh, no!" in honest simple English.

June turned away; her throat hurt as she held back tears.

She ran from the kitchen, stepped off the porch and went to her falcon. She picked him up and held him under her chin. And she stood quietly for a long, long time.

Don and Charles came out to feed Ulysses and Comet and Screamer. June sat down near Ulysses, picked a blade of grass and bit the sweet stem. "Do you believe in God?" she said simply.

Charles put one foot on a block of wood. He began, "Well, once I thought God was a big man with many ears, and thousands of eyes, and a soft body that floated over the top of the world, but—"

"I don't believe that anymore," finished Don.

"What do you believe? What's happened to Will? Who says he will die or will not?"

"No one," they both answered.

Then Charles went on, "According to the laws of nature Will is completely successful. He has produced children, and that is all that nature cares . . . that the thread of life continue."

June looked at them in surprise. "If I die now, am I deader that Will? I have no children."

June waited. She needed to know. Her brothers had read so much more than she; they had talked over so many ideas together, clearing their own thoughts through each other, that she was sure they would know the answer to death and God and the universe.

Finally Don tilted his head. "There must be something . . ." he said, "because I can't bear to know Will is dead. But I'm afraid there isn't much."

"No heaven or hell?"

"No one is really bad," said Charles.

"So there is only one place beyond life?"

"Maybe there is no place beyond life," added Don.

"Where is he then? I mean the talking and moving part that was Will?"

The brothers looked at their sister and said, "When you are sixteen you figure death a long-needed sleep."

June pondered it from her thirteen years. "A sleep? No more than that? Why does aliveness go away? Nothing else does, not the chemicals and minerals and all—only the aliveness." She looked at the twigs on the maple tree, the blue sky shining through. She stared at her falcon and her own warm hand. "I can't believe in being dead."

Charles straightened a feather on Ulysses' breast, lining up the specks. "No one can for themselves, really. Even at the last I am sure no one really believes. Maybe they know it, but they don't believe it."

June ate another piece of grass. Zander watched a beetle on a blade. Charles rubbed his hand through his hair. "I wonder what was on the other side of my life—I mean before I was born. No one has a word for that. It's not death, not heaven, not hell—I wonder what it was?"

They said no more.

They were still quiet at dinner that evening when Uncle Paul came over to taste their food and make them smile. But he wasn't hungry.

"I guess we won't hold the Falcon Hunt," Charles said. "It would be unkind since Will thought of it."

Uncle Paul took a blueberry in his brown fingers. "He

would be furious if we didn't. He was unhappy only when the excitement ended. So we'll keep the world busy and full and giving, in memoriam."

Everyone knew that was how it should be.

6. *The Falcon Hunt*

June put both feet out of bed the instant the sun brightened the top of the willow. She had decided the night before to stay in bed, very restrained, patient, exacting . . . until that moment when the light turned the purple shadow to yellow leaves. If she did this, Zander would fly to success. This was her talisman game on the dawn of the Falcon Hunt.

Then she stood before the window and saw a pink sun. There was a thread of August haze over the creek. The swallows were flocking to depart. A knock came upon the door and Rod put his head in. He was wrapped in a black piece of cloth with a pointed hat on his head. He danced through the room and out.

"Rod," she called, "who are you?"

He dashed back, "I am Merlin on the way to a Falcon Hunt! I have cast a spell. Zander will return."

"Heel squil lors (You are crazy)!"

They laughed hard and were glad about each other.

As Rod danced out, June opened her bureau drawer and for a fleeting minute wondered if she should dress up for the Falcon Hunt. She touched the green bag. It still held the paper dents where her fingernails had dug it closed. She opened it and peeked in . . . just as Don came running up the steps, and skidded to a stop at her door.

"Junie, come on! We have a surprise for you!" She kicked the drawer to close it. It stuck. She shoved. It would not budge. She spread herself awkwardly before it to hide what lay there. "I'll be along in a minute," she said. Don ran off and June looked down to see Fingers run through the door. As if a magnet were pulling him, he bounced to the drawer and climbed in. He was designed for the drawers, the closets —the dens of the house—and found them as water finds the sea. June picked him up and opened the closet to release him into that house-cave. He made contented raccoon noises as he went. "That's bigger," she said.

Then she stood over the drawer and knew she would not dress up. I don't want to wear it, she said fiercely to herself. I don't want to see people die. I want to stop growing right here. She pushed the drawer closed and as she did she tilted her head and peered in the mirror. "I wish I were beautiful, maybe then I wouldn't mind being a woman," she whispered to the glass. But the day was calling her.

She leaned out the window and yelled to her brothers, "Here I come!" Over the roof she ran to the post, climbed down, and skipped to the maple tree. She caught her breath.

There sat Zander—in a hood.

Don and Charles had been working for days on the project. They had followed an old book on falconry they had found in the Library of Congress. They had made patterns, cut fine leather, and worked out the mechanics of the falconer's tie that permitted the hunter to undo the hood with his teeth and one hand, while the other hand held the falcon. They had decorated the creation with red feathers from Uncle Paul's fishing box . . . and had led everyone to believe they were making the hood for Ulysses.

June moved as if weightless and cupped her hands like a globe around the bird. Slowly she touched the red feathers. "It isn't for Ulysses. It's too small."

Don laughed. "Well, it's sort of a reward for getting Zander trained."

She turned swiftly upon her brother, "But I don't think he is. I'm sure he'll fly away . . . and it's fall; and we leave for the city soon and . . . I don't think I'll fly him."

"Yes, you must!"

"The hood is beautiful. But I must not fly him."

Slowly she lifted the hooded bird to her finger. Zander did not move. He was alive, but dead. He sat without fluffing or making a noise. He did not even cock his head. June was frightened. "He's so . . . nothing," she said to her brothers in awe. "What's happened to him?"

"It's the hood. He's in black darkness, so he won't move. It's instinctive for the daytime birds to sit without a motion in the dark. It protects them from predators. In the dark they must be as still as a tree stub to keep from being killed. The ancient falconers found this was a good instinct to use. They could hood the birds when they carried them on horseback to hunt, and the birds wouldn't flop and break feathers. Birds are not like us; if they can't see, they don't get scared. They get calm, still, tree-stub still," said Don. "You know how Zander is when you carry him—particularly when he's hungry. He looks at everything, he's nervous, excited. He has to be that way if he's going to live by hunting. With a hood you carry him to the field quietly, and he stays quiet until you take the hood off to hunt."

"It's horrible," June said.

"It's not horrible. It's kind." Don looked at her, "Now stop feeling as if you've been blindfolded. You're not a bird. Zander likes the dark! He's calm in the dark. He doesn't hurt himself."

"Here's how you work it," Charles said. And he showed her.

June took the hood off and put it on again. "Let's get this Hunt over with," she said. "Tell everyone to come at ten instead of two."

"One thing you learn in falconry," Don said firmly, "is that nature cannot be rushed. There are inner clocks in all plants and animals and it will take another six hours before Zander and Ulysses and Comet are hungry enough to perform right. After all, we fed them yesterday morning.

They'll be hungry at ten; but they'll be eager at two. Go read a book!

"By the way, has he cast today?" Don was speaking of the neat pellet of fur and bones that all hawks and owls cast up daily about ten hours after eating. "If he hasn't, you'd better take the hood off. It makes it difficult for him to cast."

He left for a plunge in the creek, and June felt very much alone.

During lunch she practiced not being worried. She decided to live through the worst that could happen. Zander would get away, and she rehearsed, "Well, that's that." But no matter how firmly she said it, her stomach continued to churn.

And so it became two o'clock.

Down the road strode the Barneses, Emily laughing and running ahead. She came into the parlor to find June and her enthusiasm was so contagious that June ran happily to get her falcon.

Up the road came the Clarks and the Humphreys, the Sharks and the Drummers . . . and when the edge of the field was staged with people her mother looked around and said, "All Will's friends are here. This is the nicest tribute we can pay him."

Comet, the Cooper's hawk, was to fly first. Charles carried her into the field. Don opened the burlap bag and a starling flew out, zigzagging across the field in the sudden sun. Charles, his body angled like a discus thrower, threw Comet at the prey. His gauntlet was black against the sky.

The hawk beat and flashed her wings as she chased the black bird. When the starling had reached the apple orchard, the hawk broke her flight with a twist and turn of her wings, pulled and looped them among the branches. This was a flight for which a Cooper's hawk was created—chasing prey through wooded areas, maneuvering among twigs and branches. Each species of hawk is designed to hunt its food in a different area, so as not to compete with another. The Cooper's is a woodland hawk, the duck hawk needs open river beds and space, the sparrow hawk, the fields and their weedy edges.

Comet flew according to her heritage—driving relentlessly after her prey.

There was a burst of feathers . . . "Halloo" Don called, and both boys ran to the orchard after the victorious hawk. Charles picked her up and carried her across the field on his gauntlet, hand high. Comet covered her food by lifting all her feathers like a seeding thistle. Her wings spread over it protectingly. Occasionally she lifted her head to cry a warning to other predators who would stalk and take her catch. There were none, but the millions of years of her family's successful line had bred this into Comet and she could not change her heritage. Charles said, "To Will—with love," and he held the bird high.

There was a soft applause as the strong brothers came in from the field. They were brown and gold and their clothes were round and rumpled from the movement of their muscles and their vigorous way of life. They walked toward the crowd, and as they did, Uncle Paul's tears fell for the man who loved boys and birds and animals and people; and who wasn't there.

June dug her nose into Zander's back feathers so no one would see her tears. "Why is death so awfully final?"

Other eyes were wet.

Rod arose. He had abandoned his funny costume and he had brushed his hair. His shirt was soft and white. Why, Rod's handsome, June thought as she looked at him anew. Then she realized that it was Rod's compassion that was making him so appealing. He was standing beside Will's wife, and he was no longer a self-centered child, he was a growing person able to feel someone else's pain. He was sharing Mrs. Bunker's loss and he wanted her to know. Shy Rod straightened his body, lifted his head, and said to the neighbors in the field, "I've been asked to announce the flight of Ulysses, the duck hawk, falcon of the kings. Ulysses will fly in honor of . . ." and he looked down to the gray-brown woman in the grass . . . "the lady who shared Will Bunker with children and friends and animals and birds . . . Mrs. William Bunker!" His voice dropped, and he continued, "One day Will said 'there is something all life has in common, and when I know what it is I shall know myself.'" Then he sat down beside Mrs. Bunker.

Don and Charles walked into the yellow grass. Ulysses was to catch wild prey and the younger boys were called to be "beaters." They stood in a serious line at the far end of the field.

Don untethered Ulysses and threw the bird into the air, then held his pose, base wide, hands open, arms bent, as he watched the kings' bird swing up into the sky. A few neighbors arose and moved slowly into the field, for the flight of the peregrine falcon is one of the earth's most beautiful spectacles. It is perfect.

The shape of the bird against the blue sky—the long tapered wings, the streamlined body, the fanning rudder tail—was more than esthetic, it was flight, the essence of freedom to all mankind. For those in the field it was a moment of splendor. The older men, the tired middle-aged women, let themselves fly with the falcon into the unlimited sky.

The line of dusty boys moved forward. Then Don, watching the tiercel, decided he was high enough . . . some two hundred feet in the air. The bird plowed the air with his wings and "waited on." Before they had gone far a pheasant bounced from the stubble and flew up the hill.

Then, singing, singing, singing, using the earth, the air, the wind, the light—all of the world—down out of the sky came Ulysses. For an instant the sun flashed off his bending, braking feathers.

The field was still.

It was so still it was as if nothing had happened. The wind blew over the grass, the clouds flew high . . . and Mrs. Bunker arose. She said very softly but clearly, "There is no beginning or end. Life goes on and on and circling on. One life, the pheasant, sustains another life, the falcon, that sustains another life—in a mysterious, marvelous circle." She was smiling.

There was a long silence. Then Rod said, "And now let's have the spunky, fighting Zander." He flung his arm to June.

The neighbors clapped, the children jumped and bounced and called "Hooray!"

June stepped into the yellow stubble. She ran very hard up the hill to Don and handed him the motionless, hooded sparrow hawk. Then she took the lure.

Don walked bouncily down the field toward the visitors. He unleashed the falcon. As she watched him June felt her lips go dry. She could not whistle. "I'll lose him! He'll surely go," she murmured. She started down the hill to take back Zander in her hands, when Don suddenly threw him into the air. Briefly she glanced at the green and yellow and blue world . . . and she thought of Will Bunker and endings and no endings, and her thoughts went to the bird on his wings, "Either way it's all right, little fellow."

Her whistle sounded sharp and clear. Zander came on and on. He dove with shining wings in a deep dip that swept him to her lifted hand.

"Bravo!" the crowd shouted.

"Bravo!" June said to her falcon. "And now you'll learn to hunt like Ulysses. You'll be as excellent as he is. I shall work night and day to make you perfect. This I promise you."

And she walked proudly down the field.

Mrs. Bunker met her and took her hand. But June was frightened of Mrs. Bunker's tears. "It was nothing at all," she said. And she laughed. But she laughed to hide her fright. Mrs. Bunker tried to put her arm around the firm, vigorous girl. June felt the warmth and the understanding, but it was more than she could accept. She ran away, the falcon flapping to balance himself.

The services for Will Bunker were held the following day.

As soon as she arose June went without hesitation to the bottom bureau drawer and opened it. The raccoon had scattered the garments a bit, but the rumples were friendly. They gave the terribly new clothes an old, comfortable appearance.

June put on the brassiere. It was tight and hot. She twisted into the girdle then stole softly to the mirror to look at herself. For a long time she stood, and today it was suddenly all matter of fact. She leaped for her slip and the dress her mother had pressed for her the night before. As she smelled its clean freshness she said aloud, "She shouldn't have to do this work for me anymore. I can do it!" then brushed her hair and walked to the door. The back steps were near but she decided not to use them. She walked lightly to the top of the front stairs and paused. The walnut bannister gleamed in a twist to the vestibule, the white steps shone clean. She stepped down, one, then two, then three . . . on down, glowing with happiness. It was going to be lovely to be a woman.

The Falcon Hunt ended the summer. A few days later the Charles Pritchard children departed for the city and school. All winter June worked and learned and stored impressions and ideas. As new experiences came her way she longed for the water and sky of summer and long quiet hours to put them in their place. Eventually the school doors closed and the trunks were once again packed for Pritchard's.

7. *The Housekeeper*

When Charles senior kicked open the doors to the house, June ran upstairs and put her shoes under the bed without thinking. It was a habit, because she had found it was practical. She could save time by finding them quickly. She walked (last year she had leaped) to the window and looked out upon the creek with joy and excitement. Her world at fourteen was pure sun.

All winter she had been too busy to train Zander; but as she leaned far out and see-sawed on the sill, she promised on the bright water and sun and yellow flowers that she would work with him every day until he was perfect.

And she knew she would. For at fifteen, almost, June was as positive as the law of gravity.

She flew down the stairs and lifted her now brilliantly beautiful Zander from the back seat of the car to carry him across the lawn to the maple tree. Here she placed him on his old perch, wind-torn and insect-ridden. Zander had changed all his feathers during the winter and was richer in color. He was now a mature bird.

He flapped his wings, threw up his head and called "killie, killie, killie," in the manner of the male sparrow hawk telling trespassers to stay off his land. He remembered the yard at Pritchard's and was reclaiming it.

As she tethered the leash to the loop June announced to the world, "This summer you'll catch the king's breakfast!"

Her father, coming down the yard with new canoe paddles, overheard. "And what will the menu be?" he called.

"Mice tails and cricket wings on toast," she answered positively . . . "and you're the king!"

"Humph," he said with a smile. "You get that bird to hunt and I'll eat them."

"You'll see. I will." And June raced from the tree to the porch to her father. She felt like a sparkler bursting in sixty directions, for the summer was just beginning.

"I'm pretty safe," he said.

Late in the afternoon when the suitcases were unpacked and the fresh sheets spread on all the sun-aired beds, June stood before her falcon holding the lure. She whistled. Zander did not come. She whistled again and waited. It was almost dinner time when the hungry bird finally leaped on the air and winged to her hand to be fed.

"Now let's be faster tomorrow, Zander," she said.

The next night and the next night told the same tiresome story. He would not fly immediately, but sat and looked at the robins and bees.

During the winter June had handed Zander his food. Now she had to break him of expecting food without flying for it—and it was boring work. She would bring a pillow and sit in the yard, whistling and holding up her hand until it ached. She was taunted by voices laughing at the creek's edge and the sound of canoe paddles thumping gunnels. She wanted to run and play, but instead she tried to close her ears and concentrate on Zander.

"Come on, come on," she coaxed. "Please fly!" But the stubborn bird took his time. He would even lower his body, get ready to fly, and then straighten up and look at a moth in the air. After an hour he would answer her call, as he learned once again that the whistle meant food.

June was slowly understanding that to train a falcon was to play "come and be rewarded." A whistle is given, the bird flies. He is rewarded. This happens again and again, until the whistle is imprinted in his mind so deeply that when the bird hears it, without thinking "whistle equals food," he spreads his wings and answers the sound.

But to make this sequence of events possible takes, especially in a bird brain, endless practice and endless repetition —repeat, repeat, repeat, until Zander did not have to think what to do.

It occurred to June as she sat in the field whistling and

coaxing that she should have kept at the piano as faithfully as she was training Zander. She thought, I might have trained my hands until they played alone, without my head saying, "here's the note on the paper, I put it in my head, then my head tells my hands and my hands hit the key." But last year I didn't understand what they meant by "practice." It was just a nasty word designed to inconvenience and punish me. I wonder if Zander feels the same way about me?

After ten long, determined days Zander was back in flying condition. June could set him free, swing the lure, and out of the sky he would wing, to clamp his talons on the bait.

But this was only the first step. Now she must discipline him to hunt.

Charles and Don had been working, too. They made a mouse out of gray felt, and on the day Zander was to start hunting, they tied a bite of beef on it and fastened it to a long string. June tossed Zander onto his wings, then hid behind the maple tree as she pulled the felt mouse. At first the falcon in the sky looked down at June and the strange mouse. He fluttered aloft and circled the house. June whistled, the whistle brought him at once to her fist. She was disappointed that he would not strike the mouse, but thrilled again to the bird's return to her hand.

Day after day June threw Zander into the sky and pulled the mouse, with little jerky movements, across the yard. Zander tried to understand what was happening, but the routine needed to be done over and over before he could react.

"Pounce on it!" she cried to the bird above her head.

"Close your wings and come down!" The little falcon only waited on until June whistled him down.

"Haven't you any falcon sense?" she said to him one evening in utter frustration, and she shook him on her fist. He fluffed in pleasure, for her movements were not understood. To him they were the wind rocking a tree.

Then came the day June pulled the mouse across the grass—and Zander's hunting sense was aroused. He looked down from the sky, cocked his eye and put the felt toy in acute focus. Two eyes give a bird visual distance, one eye, sharp focus. So it was one eye on the mouse, then two; and Zander dropped out of the sky to bull's-eye the target.

June was thrilled. She had brought the falcon to the bait alone. Her brothers were out fishing and she could only shout to the bird her feeling of glory.

"We did it. We did it. Yippeee yi!"

And again the next day he hit the mouse, and the next. The third day Don and Charles, sitting on the porch watching like coaches at a game, arose, and huddled. They turned to June, "Time to hunt him!" they said with proud grins.

June laughed with joy, and, two-stepping in a circle, she lifted Zander overhead on her wrist.

"Let's lead the parade," she said to her falcon, and her brothers fell in behind the triumphant twosome, pleased for them both.

But the curtain on her stage of glory came down with a thump.

"Juuniee, come here at once," called her mother.

Elizabeth Pritchard was standing in the doorway of the house. Her blue dress trimmed with a white collar made her look as crisp and breathless as an autumn day. "June," she repeated, "I want to have a little talk with you."

Last year these words were ominous. They meant, time to talk about sex, or misbehavior, or some weakness of character that should be improved. They made June feel sick and uncomfortable.

This year June felt only that time for talk was time from play. She answered her mother openly, "Okay," and ran over to her, rushing too fast, nearly knocking her down as she said brusquely, "What?"

Her mother stepped back to make room for the flying girl, then led her into the parlor.

"June," she said seriously, "your father and I have decided to take a trip together into the South. We've wanted to do this for a few years, and now at last we think we can because you are old enough to run the house while we are gone. It'll be a big job, but it's time for you to take on a larger responsibility." She smiled at June and reached out a hand. "There comes a moment in every child's life when the parent says—I've driven far enough, you take the wheel for a while. Now here's the wheel." She handed June a week's menu and smiled again. "Try it—even if you fail. We'll be cheering for you. And your Aunt Helen will help you out if you run into trouble."

June had watched her brothers deliver newspapers to pay for a camera when their father had told them he would not finance it. And when they had purchased it they had looked at each other and said with glee, "We can sell pictures to buy a car to go see the West."

And one or the other had added, "And no one can tell

us what to do. It's all ours." They had smiled at their new sense of freedom.

Now it was June's turn. She was absolutely certain she could handle the job; and to prove it she asked her mother to give her a recipe for the family's favorite orange pudding. She smoothed down her hair and ran out the door.

Two days later her parents got up at dawn. Her mother fixed breakfast for them all and then departed as the purple sky turned blue. With great assurance June watched them depart, waving them down the road. When they were out of sight, she spun-jumped on Don's back.

"Whoopeee! We're all alone. What do you want to do?"

"Eat!" he answered.

"Get you to make my bed," chided Charles.

June rose to the occasion. "All right," she said brightly, "all right, I'll make your beds and I'll feed you."

She started up the steps, absolutely certain they would not take advantage of her. They followed. She waited to hear "Oh, don't." It did not come forth. She walked onto the sleeping porch. Her brothers walked behind her. They sat on the railing. June started to make Don's bed. Now, she thought, he would stop the game. Surely he would not let her do his work for him. But he said not a word. She worked on.

"Pull the sheet a little tighter, I like it smooth," he said, almost in an aside. Then added, "Please make hospital corners, too."

June finished the job and walked slowly to Charles's bed. She made it. Then with forced gaiety she asked, "Now what do you want to do?"

"Eat!" Don replied with a twinkle. June marched downstairs and made a batch of pancakes. She served them with stiff angry motions.

Charles picked one up, bent it, and as he did, he broke a pencil in his lap.

"This thing is wooden!" he said. "I don't want it."

Don put his fork into his, flipped his arm high, and kept the pancake bouncing and bouncing. He laughed, "Help, help, it's rubber!" Charles curled up in his chair in the pain of laughter—and June threw the next pancake at them.

Charles ducked, told her that was unladylike, and she had to pick it up. He chuckled to his brother. "She's mad. We'd better help her with the dishes, or we won't get any lunch."

"That's true!" June screamed.

"We're sorry." They smiled and patted her head. Then they picked up their dishes, walked out the back door, across the yard, and washed them in the creek.

"They're done!" they called. "We washed, you dry!" and they hopped into the canoe and skimmed up the creek. The plates sat on the landing. June called out in anger and in frustration, "Bring them back, please bring them back!"

Uncle Paul, who was ransacking the cupboard for breakfast food, stopped his search and walked across the floor. June could feel her shoulders shaking in her fury.

"Well, the first thing you have to learn about housekeeping is to get the human affairs in line. Why don't you call 'Thank you' and then ignore them?" June turned to him, grabbed him, and cried on his arm. Finally, she realized the possibilities of his suggestion and lifted her head. She stepped to the door.

"Thank you very much—for setting the table!" she yelled. "I'll serve your dinner there!"

"That's not being quite grown-up," he said, "but that's awfully close for an almost fifteen-year-old," and he chuckled for her side. June felt better, swished hummingly through the dishes and swept the floor.

Hands on hips, she surveyed her domain. "This is so simple," she said. "Anyone can keep house. I have hours to do nothing . . . I'll fly Zander."

Forgotten were her unmade bed and her parents'; unnoticed were three dirty cups on the table. She felt only as if she had built a pyramid.

Gently she held her hand for her falcon. He stepped on it. She closed her fingers on the jesses, untied the leash at the circlet on the ground and walked to the field with him. The sun was hot, the day so still it seemed ominous, as if a great weather change was on its way. The air was water-filled.

And yet there were only blue sky and barn swallows.

Suddenly there were no barn swallows. They spotted the falcon the moment June stepped into the field. They gave their thin high cry "danger, danger, danger, danger" and vanished from sight.

Far out in the mowed alfalfa, far away from the house and the brooms and the dishes, June threw her bird onto his wings. He climbed the sky.

"All right. Let's try it. You're on your own!" she called to him.

She held her arms back and out, placed her feet wide on the earth and watched the falcon fly. He fanned first one wing against a wall of air, then the other, dug into the sky as if his wings were canoe paddles and swept straight up, up, up.

As he climbed, June went with him. She felt the wind in her face, the draughts and gusts of the air avenues, the lightness of her body. As Zander circled high above the field he darted like a wind-blown leaf, stopped, plowed the air with his wings, and waited on! He stood still above her. He scooped the air with the tips of his feathers so that he did not go forward or backward. He stood in the sky, waiting for the game to be stirred.

June stood transfixed in the yellow-green field. With her head back, her arms slightly lifted, she stared at the waiting bird.

What are we doing, beautiful falcon? she said to herself. Are we talking to each other? Why, why, why are you doing as you were told?

June's world was white and yellow as she beheld with wonder the miracle of what she was about. She too was of the earth. She was part of its green grass, its water to drink, its air in her lungs . . . and for joy, its wild birds above her head. Like a blade of grass, like a flying bird, June knew she was no less, nor any more, than the earth and the sun that she came from.

And she was glad to be part of it, and part of the bird that waited on. She ran, he followed. She circled, he circled. She went backward, he went backward.

Realizing that he was depending on her earth-boundness

to help him, she rushed through the cut clover and alfalfa to stir a mouse. None skipped out. She circled wide. The bird circled wide. She found a stick and beat. Once she looked up at him. His eyes were riveted to the twist of her hair in the wind, the flash of her feet—to every movement she made.

"What do you see?" she shouted. "The petals on the timothy? The antennae on the butterfly? Is everything very sharp and detailed in your keen, keen eyes?"

The bird moved forward a foot, plowed the air, and waited. June laughed to him. Then she ran back and forth up the hill.

She ran faster and faster. With a burst, a sparrow, feeding in an open spot in the hayfield, shot into the air.

The blue sky streaked with the falcon, coming down so fast she almost missed his descent. He had pumped twice on high, turned his head earthward, and fallen. He dropped toward the life that would die to give him life. Feathers burst from the prey like the dandelion in the wind. And the song of the earth was repeated as one life became another life.

June ran to Zander. He, like other falcons, was covering his prey. As she came closer he raised the feathers on top of his head and moved a shoulder over his food. His actions said, "This is mine." June respected his feelings, and she spoke to him softly, "I don't want it. I don't want it," then lifted him carefully off the ground and held him on her fist. The warm sparrow breast was against her hand. Zander, at home on the lifted hand, relaxed his feathers, stopped covering, and stared at June brightly.

"There! All on a sunny day we know the secret of life," she said to the black-eyed, red-backed bird. "Now, if I liked sparrows and clover, you and I could live forever in this field. I would build us a grass hut to protect us from the storms. You would catch food for us and we would need no more." She paused and added wistfully, "except . . ."

"Bravo!" came a cry from the edge of the field. "We saw him do it!"

June spun to see Don and Charles, fishing poles in their hands, running over the hay stubble toward her.

"It was great! Perfect! Beautiful!"

"Don't feed him but a small bite. We want to get movies." They ran back to the house, their brown legs bowing at the knees.

During the past winter the twins had become expert photographers with their hard-won camera. They used the birds and pets around them as subjects. National magazines had bought their pictures and their articles as they began at seventeen to work out their careers. Now they were being called upon to lecture with movies, and the story of the first flight of a falcon was just the tale they wanted their cameras to tell. Both came hurrying back to fill the field with tripods, hoods, lenses, cameras—and argument. When Don and Charles worked together they argued, loud, long—as a person argues with himself when he comes to a decision. Their mother often shouted, "Stop arguing," and they would look up and say, "Who's arguing? I'm not arguing. I'm thinking out loud."

For the rest of the morning they worked long and hard.

Zander performed beautifully, catching first a mouse (the film ran out and he had to do it again) and then a shrew. On the second kill he flew right into the camera and flashed the undersides of his wings—black and white—so that the sun bent off them as if they were gems.

As Zander hovered over his food, and the camera clicked out the climax of the young falcon's first hunt, Don said, "Wow. I'm starved!"

"Oh!" June said. "I'm supposed to be cooking something."

"Just get some sandwiches," Charles called as she ran toward the house. "Cook the big meal tonight. We want to get Zander being carried home in his hood."

She ran all the way to the kitchen, put bread, butter, and jelly together hastily, and ran all the way back. The twins were loading cameras. She passed her offerings. Don bit deep into one, chewed and turned suddenly upon her. "What the devil is in this?"

"Jelly," she answered, worried. "Why?"

"You're not trying to get even with us for leaving the dishes at the canoe landing, are you?"

"Oh, no," she said, and watched in fascination as he slowly pulled his sandwich out of his mouth, spewed the contents, and turned it over for inspection.

"These are pure blue sandwiches," he said, and thrust the mess at her. The bread was feathery with summer mould.

"I'm sorry," she said, "I'll make some more." Startled that her job wasn't going according to her mental picture of an easy, smooth week, she was eager to run back to the house and try again. But the twins only wanted to get on with their work.

"Never mind, we'll go down to the store and buy some candy bars," Charles said gloomily, and reached into his blue jeans, found some change, and led them down the road. He had enough money for ice cream cones as well. They walked quietly back to the field to finish the movie.

When the last of the short story of the falcon was filmed they went to the creek for a swim with Rod, feeling grand for having accomplished something, and therefore loud and silly. They splashed and dived and called to each other.

"June!" yelled Rod. "Get the other end of the seine, and let's troll the bottom of the creek." She burst out of the water and joined him.

She was feeling independent now. No one would call her to work. She was happy about her falcon and ready for a treat. The timing on the housework was up to her.

The seine and the bottom of the stream fascinated them. It made them laugh hard and long. And June needed to laugh, she needed a party mood to celebrate her pride in her bird, and the silly stream bottom seemed just right. She took the other end of the net and followed Rod into the meadow where they began their hunt.

In one dip they brought up all manner of marvelous life from the swift waters and the rocks. There were crayfish, hellgrammites, the dragonlike larva of a fly. There were stone flies in cases made from their saliva and tiny bits of sand, and each had a trap door which opened and closed. Rod held one in the swift water until it opened and June giggled at the clownlike face that poked out. Then Rod touched the door and it closed.

"Spil squid," he commented. June giggled again.

"Spil fors," she laughed.

"Spil predjow." They both curled with hysterics.

"Rod," she finally said, "why are you so wise and foolish?"

"Because I am misunderstood," he said. "I do not want to grow up at all. I want to grow out." They laughed again.

June saw that the shadows were long. She stood up suddenly. "It's late! I've got to start supper." Rod picked up the seine and they ran through the bouncing bets, across the floodgates that carried the water to the flour mill, and home. Aunt Helen was at the edge of the porch calling her own family to the table for dinner. June hurried to her room, dressed and, bright-hearted, stood before the kitchen table.

"I think I'll bake a cake," she said with cheer. One of her chores during the winter was to bake a cake every Saturday. She was very good at it.

She creamed the butter and the sugar, and was adding the egg and flour when it occurred to her that she ought to have the water boiling for the potatoes. She lit the wick on the kerosene stove, filled a pot and placed it over the fire. Then she went back to the cake. Now, have I put in two cups or one? she asked herself. It looked runny so she added another cup—and remembered, too late, that it needed only half a cup. She added a little more milk.

She could hear the potato water boiling.

"I haven't peeled the potatoes," she said in disgust, and

rushed to the cupboard for them. There was no water to wash them in. She got water and began the job. And then she remembered that a pork roast takes a long time to cook.

She stopped peeling potatoes and took the roast from the icebox. She found the salt, salted and peppered the roast and ground garlic over it as a good French chef once taught her mother to do. Then she got the oven ready and put in the roast.

She finished peeling the potatoes, put them in the water which had now boiled low, and went back to the cake.

She added the rest of the ingredients, greased the pan, and poured the batter, gold and flowing, into the pan. When she had carried the cake to the oven she saw that she could not get both the cake and the roast in the small space. She could feel a wave of desperation break over her and would have thrown herself on the green chair and kicked her heels—except that she didn't have the time.

She had to think.

Knowing that the cake would go flat, she took the roast out and put the cake in. Then she smelled something and wondered if the boys were burning bird feathers. The smell was coming from the stove. The potatoes were burned.

She peeled some more while she waited for the cake to bake. She peeked in the oven and noticed that it was not rising. She had left out the baking powder. Out came the cake and in went the roast.

The cake dripped as she poured it in the garbage. She tried to get the burn off the potato pan.

And then the twins came in.

"Hey, is dinner ready?" they said brightly and trustingly. "We're starved."

She thought she was calm, but when she spoke her voice squeaked, "No! It's not ready!" Then in a low tone, she added, "You'd better fly Ulysses or something; it'll be another hour."

Two hours later the meat was roasted, the potatoes were stone cold, and she had not shelled the peas.

Don and Charles insisted upon eating. "Make gravy and that will heat up the potatoes. We don't need peas. We'll eat lettuce."

She began to make gravy, adding flour as she stirred. The mixture was too thick. She added water . . . too thin, added flour. Too thick, too thin.

Her brothers sat on Aunt Helen's table swinging their feet and watching, saying nothing, just swinging their feet harder every time she added either the flour or the water. When she finished she had almost a gallon of gravy —as Don observed.

Said Charles, "That'll do for a month." And he curled over and laughed. "Let's eat."

Don carried the roast into the parlor and placed it on the round table.

As he sat down he asked, "What are we going to eat on? Red gingham squares?" She had forgotten to set the table.

She ran around the table and put down plates, then ran back to the kitchen for spoons and ran round the table putting them down, next the knives, the forks, the napkins.

"Can't you do that from one spot all at once?" asked Don, and took the silverware from her hands and placed it on the table, chuckling to himself. She wanted to dig her elbow in him, but she knew if she did she would burst into tears. She hurried to the icebox for milk.

Charles sat in his father's seat and served. He folded his napkin in his lap, helped himself to potatoes, heated them with hot gravy, and passed the lettuce. He flicked his elbows, cut a bite of meat, and put it in his mouth. He coughed and swallowed hard.

"What is this? Roast garlic?"

"Oh, don't tease me now," said June, "I'm about to cry."

"I'm not teasing, taste it."

It was awful. Don managed to find enough meat in the very center to get one garlic-free serving apiece.

Don made some helpful remark about how he'd been taught that a cook could get the right amount of garlic in food by letting the shadow fall upon it. Charles laughed, June looked helpless. They found enough tasty food, however, to "sustain life," as Don worded it.

After drying the dishes June crawled up the back steps, feeling her exhausted way to her room. She took off only her shoes and socks, then pulled up the covers and felt the sweet comfort of the pillow.

As she was falling asleep she heard the sleeping-porch door open, then footsteps along the hall. Don and Charles were sneaking down the back steps.

"Whatcha doing?" she called.

"Going down to get peanut butter sandwiches. We're starved!"

She was too tired to cry. She just murmured, "And Zander became trained in only three weeks."

8. The Flood

At midnight, her uncle rapped on June's door.

"We're in for a big storm, Junie—wind and lots of water. The hurricane that hit Virginia yesterday is here. Put on your bathing suit and bring in your falcon!"

June was awake and on her feet. Outside she could see the willows bend and the underside of the sycamore leaves shine silver as the storm tossed them. The night sucked and shook and blew. The earth was on violent terms with itself.

Everybody was up.

She dashed into the wind. It snatched the breath from

her throat and snapped her hair like whips against her face. Zander, Zander . . . he could not withstand this. He would be torn from his perch, pulled the length of his jesses, then yanked to his death. She ran across the yard, head down, into the driving, painful rain.

Her falcon was on his perch. She was amazed to see him, facing the storm, eyes half-closed. She cupped him in both hands and tried to lift him. He held tight. She pulled again, his talons dug in. He could not let go. The more she pulled, the tighter he gripped. He was designed to stay alive in a world of storm and stress, and the harder the wind blew, the more June pulled, the tighter the tendon in his rear toe grasped the perch. She remembered the night her father had told her about this tendon. They were watching Zander as he slept. When he settled down and relaxed, the tendon in the back of his leg clamped his toes shut. Now he stood in the storm because his legs were bent in the position that locked his toes on his perch. She released him, his toes opened, and she snatched him up quickly before he could grab again. She ran into the house, slammed the door and leaned against it. The downstairs hall was in a state of motion as Don came in with Ulysses, Charles with Comet; and Rod called out the door for Bobu.

Charles saw his sister hugging her wet cold bird to her chest.

"Spread newspapers at the far end of the living room," he shouted. "We'll put the birds on Aunt Helen's side and the animals on ours."

Aunt Helen came down the stairs and sleepily sat on the couch. She watched "the creatures come aboard the ark."

"Ulysses looks splendid on the cherry chair," she observed, as the noble falcon stood straight and drew up a yellow foot. To June the needlepoint on the chair seemed more rich in color for the falcon's presence. Slowly he lifted his feathers. They ventilated him in the heat and cold, keeping him comfortable no matter the temperature. The feathers puffed out at the bottom of his breast, then stood out like thistledown over his crop. Those on the top of his head, around his ears, his eyes, and finally his nares, were the last to stand softly ajar. He was gentle-looking and exquisite.

Comet was placed on the back of a dining-room chair nearby. The bird stared at the new surroundings, decided they would not harm her, and relaxed. Bobu, wet and sodden, flew to the turntable on the victrola. He shook.

The two new hawks of the season were tethered to fireplace logs placed in the middle of the floor. They were a red-tailed hawk named Leviticus and a marsh hawk named Ponderous. The red-tailed and marsh hawks would never make good hunters. They were slow, soaring birds; but Don and Charles were raising them because, having learned to train falcons, they wanted next to know more about other birds of prey. They were curious to discover how hawks fit into the scheme of nature, why the woodlot had one kind of bird, the marsh another kind, the seacoast still another.

When the birds were settled, Don put Fingers, the raccoon, in a barrel on their mother's side of the house. Then Jim came in with Tabu, his pet of the summer—an undescented skunk. He was put in a box. The skunk and the raccoon were good friends, they sported and played outside. But this was the first time they had been together in a small space. All watched breathlessly to see what would happen.

Hardly had Jim put Tabu on the floor than Fingers cavorted, bounced, pranced to meet him. Tabu chuttered a small frightened greeting. The house was strange, the winds had been unnerving. Tabu was not in a mood to play. He threw up his tail to halt the silly creature coming toward him.

Fingers ducked his coon head, threw high his hind feet, then snatched the beautiful black and white skunk tail and pulled it down. Quickly Tabu turned upon him, horseshoed his body and aimed to fire. "Get that coon!" shouted Charles. And Jim stuffed Tabu in the fireplace and put the screen up.

Suddenly, they heard a call from the other side of the house. Ulysses had his talons in Leviticus. Don separated them.

Charles turned out the lights. All the birds sat still, motionless on chairs and blocks of wood, as if they were in hoods.

But the skunk and raccoon on the other side of the house did not react to the darkness like the birds. They were animals of the night. The darkness awakened them to activity. No sooner were the lights off than Fingers began to scramble out of the barrel and Tabu pushed the fire screen aside. In seconds Fingers landed on the frightened Tabu—and spray arose through the house. Up, up, the steps; up, up, to the top of the high ceilings and through the stove-holes; up, up to the attic went the fumes.

And then with a shivering blast, the shutters rattled, the storm came down upon a window-shut, blind-fastened house. For five minutes the smell was dreadful. It pained eyes and noses. June felt as if she would suffocate and go blind.

After a while Don observed wonderingly, "I can't smell anything anymore. Can you, June?"

"Phew, yes," and she sniffed hard, "well, on the second sniff . . . no!"

"It's so horrible that it seals off the smelling buds in your nose so you can't smell anymore. It protects you," said Charles. "I'm sure the house smells but we can't smell it." They were starting off to bed when Aunt Helen called, "The creek is rising fast, I can't see the canoe landing!"

They burst through the back door and ran down the yard. The landing was there, but under an inch of water, and the creek was boiling and rising swiftly.

As they went into the house they were overcome by skunk scent, and decided they would endure it by going to bed. It was all right as long as they lived with it. "That's why a skunk can live with himself," Rod concluded.

The next morning June got up at seven, determined to get the day off to an orderly start. She rushed to the dining room, set the table, and served everyone cold cereal and milk. It filled them up, and there were no remarks. Then and there she planned and began the mid-day meal. She peeled potatoes, made hamburger patties, shelled peas, got two pots and one frying pan going, put the potatoes on to boil first because they took the longest, then the peas, then the meat; she looked out the door at the storm and set the table.

And everything was done and hot at once . . . at 10 A.M.!

She found Don and Charles making falcon hoods in the living room with Jim. Rod was spinning Bobu on the victrola and Aunt Helen was playing "Rustles of Spring" on the piano. June walked among them, head high, and said, as if it were the most natural thing in the world, "Dinner is served!" There was a stunned silence.

She added, "And it's all hot."

Charles arose and walked slowly over the newspapers to the door, and across the hall to the parlor. He returned to say, "So help me, it is." Upon which June burst into tears and ran to Zander. She stared into his ebony eyes and noticed the fine brown lines in his iris. Details seemed important just then.

Rod, watching from the side of the room, jumped to the floor and said, "Heel squil flid! Heel bull squirm (I'm starved. I've got worms)!"

He ran across the hall and pounced upon a chair.

"Whatever he said, I get the idea. I'm hungry too," said Charles.

Charles removed Fingers, who had abandoned his barrel for the odors on the table, and was helping himself to hamburgers. He locked him in the pantry and placed himself gallantly at the head of the table. Don joined them.

They ate almost all morning, jumping up now and then to run around the table and make more room for the next bite; getting the weather map out and following the path of the storm; taking umbrellas and running down the yard to see how high the water was; coming back for another mouthful.

By noon the dinner was almost gone. Then Uncle Paul, having finished oatmeal and pie on his side of the house half an hour earlier, came over and sat down to a mound of potatoes, peas, and the last two hamburgers. He ate very slowly, and chewed long and swallowed hard. June laughed and cried and hugged him and said, "I love you. You understand people."

"But it's delicious!" he exclaimed and forced down a bite. "And you know how I love delicious food."

"Is it?" she asked.

"It sure is!"

The creek kept rising. It passed the sycamore and elm. June spent the afternoon in the attic, rummaging through boxes of old books. The attic was lined with sets of Dickens, Tolstoy, Turgenev, Emerson, Thoreau in endless boxes.

Furthermore, in the attic she could watch the flood, hear the rain beat the slate, and see the mud daubers— slender wasps—build their communal pueblos. And it was here that she had her most private thoughts.

That night everyone went to bed again still listening to the rain. They awoke to wind and water; but at noon, when June was adding more milk to the too thick white sauce for creamed tuna on toast, she heard Don come splashing over the millstone at the back porch to announce the sun.

She stopped stirring and stepped out the door. To the

south the sun flickered through racing clouds. The rain had ceased. The storm clouds were circling north.

"Oh, beautiful," she cried.

The stream was as brown as gravy and as thick. Sticks and leaves churned in it. Don and June stood enthralled as they looked out on the muddy dashing flood. An expensive canoe landing with benches and green paint leaped along on the waters. It was followed by a chicken coop with two chickens sitting upon it.

Rod called from his parents' bedroom window, "What a ride we'd get on that water!"

"You said it," Don answered. "We'd go down the creek faster than a motorboat if we jumped in."

"Hey, let's try it!" said June suddenly. Her joy at seeing the sun, her excitement at beholding the mighty river at her door, inspired her to action. She ran back and plopped the lumpy sauce on the table and turned off the kerosene stove. The boys passed her as they ran for their bathing suits, but June changed to hers and still caught up with them at the front door. As she passed the living room Uncle Paul called, "June, wait a minute, did you feed Zander?"

"Yes," she answered. She started to run on.

"Did you?" he asked again.

She had not. But she couldn't stop now, she *had* to get into that fast, exciting water right away.

"Of course I did!" she answered.

"Okay then. We'll unleash him and put him in the ash tree. He'll stay there since he's fed. He and Bobu need sun. Their feathers are dull. Besides, I want to clean the house of the newspapers and mess the creatures have caused."

June moved back to stop him from taking Zander, but dared not. She had to play out the lie she had told. Briefly she was frightened, then remembering how well Zander was trained she called back confidently, "Okay, put him out."

The idea of riding the swift flood became more and more irresistible. June joined the high-pitched chatter as the young Pritchards slipped away from the house without telling their uncle of their intentions. At the iron bridge they met Emily and Bill Barnes. They, too, jumped at the idea of swimming in the speeding waters.

Don started off. He waded out to the submerged bridge, ran up the slanting iron bar to the top and stood there like a mountain sheep.

"Heck, it's only ten feet to the water!"

He made a soaring dive and disappeared under the roiling mud-water. Charles dove in next, then Rod.

June hesitated a moment on the bridge top as she looked over the countryside at the sea of water that lapped at houses and barns. The dive was more than she wanted to do. Suddenly the whole project seemed ridiculous, but it was too late to let that thought get anywhere. There was really only one choice to make, whether to jump or dive. She jumped.

As she came up for air she saw the Heffelfinger's tool shed pass her. Then she saw Emily and her brother bobbing on the flood. Laughter rang out as they churned downstream.

Suddenly, opposite the Pritchard house, was a sheet of

curling water. She heard a voice shout, "The railroad bridge! Duck and go under! You can't go over! Pass it on!"

She called to Emily.

"The railroad bridge! Duck and go under! You can't go over! Pass it on!" and then dove deep.

When she was sure she had passed under the bridge she ruddered upwards and came bursting onto the crest that was the dam—twelve feet below. The others followed safely. Then, lifting one arm like a silly clown, June swam thirty feet per stroke. It was marvelous! She stroked again and passed the fishing hole. Arms flayed, voices rose to high C, the creek roared—and life was close to death.

At the sycamore tree where she and Rod had seined the week before, she took Don's hands. He pulled her out of the water and signaled her to lie on her stomach and reach for the next swimmers.

"If we go any farther," he shouted, "we won't stop until Boiling Springs."

Happily and with gusto they collected all the flood-riders on the sycamore limbs. Don led the way through tree tops to the quiet waters, the shallows, and finally the earth. They jumped on the sod and ran all the way back to the iron bridge to dive again.

This time they were so sure of themselves that they improvised silly strokes and made jokes as they roared along on the flood.

The third time they were nonchalant.

As June gleefully swam past the house at Pritchard's, she looked up to see Zander above her. Hungry Zander was not sitting in the sun. He had heard June laughing and calling on the flood and he had flown to her for food. He fluttered above her head and as she reached to shoo him back to land, someone called, "Dive under for the railroad bridge!"

She dove, and when she came up at the dam she looked back to see if Zander was all right. Her well-trained bird had tried to alight on her lifted hand, and she feared he might have dipped too low, got his wings wet, and become too heavy to fly. He was nowhere to be seen.

She clutched at a willow and held on. The rush of the water pushed her under, but she struggled to her feet and worked through an adjacent willow to an oak to a maple to the floodgates. There she swam in the quiet backwater, waded ashore, and ran back to the railroad bridge where she had last seen Zander. As she came through the yard she saw her mother and father drive in. She waved but did not stop, for she had to find her falcon. She whistled; there was no reply. She called. She ran up and down the railroad tracks and whistled and shouted. Then she wept, for she knew Zander would come back if he were alive.

But calling and whistling made her feel better, so she ran on and on, nearer and nearer the main channel. And then she noticed a different kind of movement in all the downward motion of the flood. This one jerked. It was on a grapevine near the railroad track. It was Zander, immersed in water, flapping his wings and holding to a twig by the hook of his beak.

"I'm coming!" she cried, and jumped into the water to swim across the bergamot garden to the backwater where

Zander held precariously. She picked him up and lifted him high, treading water as she went up the yard to the ash tree. There she crawled out and struggled into the kitchen with the half-dead bird. Her mother and father were talking to her uncle and aunt.

"Hey," her father said, "aren't you glad to see us?"

"Yes, of course, of course, I guess. But I almost lost Zander." She was placing the bird in a soft towel to dry him. He hardly struggled.

Life in a bird is touch and go. A wet body can be death. Her father kicked open the coal stove that heated the water. "Hold him close to the fire," he said. "He must not lose body heat."

June crept to the red coals, but Zander was too wet, too stiff. "Give him to me," her father said gently. "Birds can be motionless and as cold as the grave, and warmth will revive them." Sobbing so hard her throat hurt, June put Zander in his hand.

Her father blew on the bird, held him to the fire, turned him over, tapped him on the head, and worked with him for what seemed an eternity. Finally June saw the feathers lift. Her father said very quietly, "He blinked an eye. You can take him now. Keep him warm."

For another hour June held him close to the warmth, drying each intricately beautiful feather, and when supper was ready, Zander was sitting perkily on her finger.

Uncle Paul came over to stroke the bird. "I can't figure out what happened," he said. "He was fed. He should have sat still. None of the others went off the tree."

"I don't know," June muttered.

"If you hadn't fed him I would have understood. You did feed him, didn't you?" her uncle insisted.

"Yes," she whispered.

And now a second lie had cut off her next move to help the bird. She did not dare go to the icebox for meat for the dangerously hungry falcon. If she did, her first lie would be out. It was so much simpler to be honest.

"Put Zander outside," her father said, "and come eat."

"Please," she begged. "He needs to be warm. Let me keep him in my room."

"No, he's all right now. He's fine. I want him out of the house."

"Please, please, please, you must! You must!" And she carried Zander to her room. Even if she was to be punished, she had to do this.

She waited until she knew everyone would be in the kitchen washing his hands for dinner, then she stepped out her window onto the porch roof, slid down the post and ran to the parlor window under which the icebox sat.

She had to move fast. She climbed in the window, went to the icebox and opened it. There was no wild food. She rummaged until she found some uncooked stew meat, snatched a piece, crawled out the window, and ran back to the porch post. But she could not climb it. Her mother was at the back door. And she was angrily talking to Charles and Don about the flood.

"Did June go swimming with you?"

"Oh, sure," said Don.

"June!" her mother called.

June knew she was trapped. She wondered whether to

answer from the porch or her room. She decided on the room and shinnied up the post, ran across the roof, climbed in her window, and called downstairs, "Whattee?"

"What are you doing?" came her mother's know-it-all-anyway voice.

"Getting dressed." The third lie.

June heard her mother start up the steps to see what was going on. June slammed the screen on the window, skinned out of her bathing suit, and was at her closet when her mother came folded-armed into her room.

"Now what is all this climbing in and out of windows? What have you done? What's this meat doing up here?" She picked up the blob June had dropped on the bed when she had hurried to dress.

"Come downstairs. I want to talk to you and your brothers."

June walked down slowly, dreading each step.

"You hadn't fed that bird, had you, June?"

"No," she whispered. "Please let me! Please, please, his wings are drooping, his feathers are lifted as if he's sick. I did lie. Please, let me feed him."

She ran back up the stairs, surprised at how simple the truth made her mission. She fed her falcon with easy heart.

"Goodness," she said, "it's not that lying is evil, it's so cumbersome and unworkable."

The bird gulped. June lifted him to her finger, huddled him against the warmth of her throat. "I get mixed up," she told him. Zander cocked an eye at her. She carried him downstairs to help her face the next issue—the flood.

There was no getting out of anything now. Her mother and father were waiting. The twins were standing quietly side by side.

Her mother began sternly, "You've abused your freedom. You didn't use your privileges properly. You got heady with the lack of restrictions and endangered your lives. Don and Charles, you're both older. You should have used your training *to think*. As for you, June, I shall keep you home and train you further. Now go to your rooms and think about this. Freedom is dangerous, unless you can stand up to its demands."

Their father, standing on the balls of his feet lightly, looked toward the creek. "We're glad you're all alive . . . including Zander. Please bring your brains and enthusiasm together in more fruitful ventures."

As June passed him on her way to the stairs she struck out once more, "Oh, I wish I didn't ever have to decide by myself what to do. I never seem to make the right decisions."

Her mother smiled at her. "Growing up is a long process of needing things and not needing things, like mothers and fathers and birds. Then finally, one day, you find you can make a big decision happily and with conviction. That's what we call maturity. Someday, maybe in a summer or two you'll come together in one piece—your head and your feelings." She flicked off the porch light, and her heels snapped across the linoleum.

June stood alone, running her hand over the black-eyed falcon. "What on earth is she talking about?" she whispered to the sleepy bird.

9. *The Meet*

The flood waters retreated in jerks and starts like a sleeping dog pulling out of the hot sun. By the afternoon of the next day the canoe landing was in view. All the young Pritchards were sent to dig off the gluey mud.

Said Don, "Hey, Dad was really mad at us for riding the flood. I've never seen him so angry."

"Oh, well," said Rod, "he and my dad are pretty old. They got mad because they can't do it."

June thought a moment. "No," she said firmly, "they were mad because they feel they have to restrict us—they just want to boss! . . . Whee! It was marvelous."

They chuckled in cheery comradeship.

"Do you think you'll ever do it again?" she asked them. "Now that Dad and Mother are so mad?"

They answered as one, "Oh, sure!"

Then Charles said, "Dad did worse things than that when he was young. He ran over the iced creek on a winter day so he wouldn't have to go to Sunday School—and fell through. He walked under the ice until he came to a hole he knew about and got up. Wasn't scared a bit for the same reason we weren't. He knew what he was doing. But now? Well, he's a father, and you know how fathers are. Their parents got mad at them, so they get mad at us, and I guess we'll get mad at our children—that's how it goes."

June was still unsatisfied. "Well, why did Mother make such a funny punishment for me: stay home and learn to use my freedom by cooking and keeping house? I'm never going to get married anyway. Babies have cereal all over their faces and are much too much trouble."

"I'll bet she's been thinking about that trip to England you could have taken this summer. You know, the one with the bikes and the kids camping from London to Scotland."

June had forgotten. It had all sounded wonderful until she had thought about leaving her parents, her brothers, and her falcon. Then she grew stomach sick and knew she could not.

"I guess you're right. She's trying to make me sensible when I'm on my own."

"Well, she wants you to stand on your own two feet when you're off in the world," Don said.

"But I'm afraid to go, sort of."

"Why?"

"Well, I'm afraid to be nasty—suppose some man tries to love me—or something."

"Oh, Junie. The devil with that. You don't have to do anything you don't want to do. Nothing. You're the captain of yourself, and everyone respects the captain."

"I guess so."

"I know so. You don't have to be afraid."

"Suppose I like it? I'm afraid of that, too."

"Well, then, you just remember that your body is pretty dumb. It can't see, and has a short memory—so you turn the decision over to your head. Your head will be planning your future."

"I see." She didn't really, but she was impressed with his wisdom.

Jim came running down the yard. He jumped onto the muddy landing and slid from one end to another, handing Don a letter as he passed.

"It's from India!" he said in excitement. "For Masters Charles and Don Pritchard, Esquire. Wow!"

Don opened the letter. "It's from that Indian prince who wrote us last spring. He's named 'Bapa.' That means 'younger son' in Hindustani, he told us."

"Bapa," said Rod. "What a great combination of sounds. I wish I had thought of that. Bapa."

"Hey, Junie, let's call a 'game' a 'bapa.' I haven't a word for game."

"Listen to this!" Don read aloud, " 'I have read again of your falcons about which you wrote with great interest in the national magazine. I wonder if you brothers match your falcons in combat as the Rajah, my brother, and I do? Each morning before breakfast we match our best falcons in chase, to see which brings home the most food for our table. I would like to hear which of your falcons wins. I have only thirty falcons and thirty men to train them at this time.

" 'God willing, someday you will come to see me or I will come to see you. Your friend, Bapa.' "

"God willing, we had better go see him first," Charles exclaimed. "Thirty falcons and thirty men to train them . . . and me with only three."

"Four," June said. "Zander counts."

"And we've never matched one against the other," said Don. "Yes, God had better be willing to get us to India first."

"Well, in case He isn't," Rod said with great practicality, "maybe we could have a little falcon match here and get in shape for Bapa. I don't know why Zander couldn't match Ulysses. You wouldn't have to count size in the contest, just numbers. If Zander gets more mice than Ulysses gets pheasants, he wins."

Charles roared, "Yeah, yeah! This will be a new kind of falcon match, an American type of falcon match entitled, 'To Each His Own.' "

"Or," said Don, "the falcon match to prove that all birds are created equal."

"Well, let's go!" said Jim. "I hereby announce the All-American Falcon Match!" He poked a broom into the air and marched off the landing and up the yard. Rod joined him, swinging the bucket, and June lifted the shovel and followed.

Uncle Paul who had been cleaning mud off the tool shed floor, poked his head out and called, "When that landing is clean, you hunt falcons, and not before!"

Rod turned the parade back, mumbling, "My father is nice—BUT."

That "but" marked the beginning of her parents as real people for June. Rod had challenged the perfection of his father. It was a shock. June lifted her head and looked toward Uncle Paul. He seemed a little less austere. She thought about her own father and mother. Maybe they were right about the flood, and maybe they were not. She straightened up from mopping and grinned to herself. By doubting them, her own faults seemed more tolerable.

So they finished the mud-clearing quickly and carried Ulysses and Zander to the field late in the afternoon.

Their father and uncle followed, intrigued with the idea that two falcons with two different ways of life were going to vie with each other. Charles senior, a naturalist by profession, respected this broadening of his sons' interest in falconry. Uncle Paul joined the trip because it was another imaginative venture with people and animals. Since Will Bunker's death, adventure had lost its pranklike aspect for Uncle Paul and had become more "how to learn," although it never lacked spirit and humor.

Everyone sensed they were off to some high adventure this day as they played an old Indian game with American rules. There was bounce in their steps.

June carried the hooded Zander on her fist, confident that

he would catch more sparrows and mice and crickets than Ulysses would catch pheasants and pigeons.

The summer was well into goldenrod and Queen Anne's lace. As they walked to the field they scared up several groundhogs and two or three rabbits.

"Why are there so many animals today?" June asked her father. They were walking together companionably, June quietly happy in his presence.

"The young animals of the season are reaching puberty," he said. "They are being sent off by their parents to seek their fortunes and set up new homes. It's a bad time for the young. A lot of them get killed. They are shoved out of their homes, they don't know the hiding spots in the new areas, and they blunder. They run in the open because they don't know the trails, and hawks, foxes, owls catch them. They cross unfamiliar roads, and cars kill them."

He looked around. "There are wild hawks and falcons here. They know the fields are filled with careless children of the wilderness, and are hunting this easy-to-catch food."

In the middle of the field, Ulysses was sent aloft. The men kicked through the grasses. Almost immediately two spry young pheasants of the year burst out.

Ulysses dropped out of the sky and took one of them.

"Hooray!" shouted Don and Charles, grinning with victory.

The duck hawk was retrieved and the bird taken from him. He would be fed later. Now it was important to keep him hungry for the competition.

Next Zander went up in the sky. June did not fear this

time that she would lose him. Her only anxiety now was that he might not win.

The young mice of the year, out seeking their fortunes, were as careless as her father predicted. Soon Don kicked up a family, and Zander bulleted out of the sky to tie the score.

"Tallyho!" she shouted.

Ulysses was thrown off. While Charles tried to find him food he suddenly came down on a pigeon flying from the barn to the nearby granary. Again the boys hoorayed, and ran far out in the field to bring back the fleet-winged tiercel.

Zander went aloft and waited on until June feared he would drop of exhaustion. No small birds were flying. No young mice were rushing into openings. Suddenly Zander plummeted from the sky and disappeared into the purple blooms of the alfalfa.

"It counts!" shouted Don. "He dove, and that counts. So it's Ulysses two, Zander one!"

June was furious. "It doesn't count," she shouted. "There wasn't anything to catch. There has to be something, or it doesn't count!"

She continued to argue with them as she backed to the spot where Zander had disappeared.

"Yes, it does!" said Charles, siding with Don.

And June continued to shout, "No, no, no!"

With flashing suddenness, a red-tailed hawk appeared overhead. He was winging from the woods at the edge of the field, where he had been watching the contest. He dove, and with horror June saw him plunge on the spot where Zander sat.

She shouted and waved her hands, but there was a hundred yards between herself and the big hawk. Intent upon his mission, he saw nothing but food fluttering in the grass.

The boys burst behind her, shouting and waving their arms as they responded to the crisis. Suddenly Charles took off his shoe. He stood very still, aimed, and hurled it at the hawk.

The shoe clipped the big bird. He veered off. His wing beats rippled the grass as he flew to the apple orchard.

Zander was unharmed. He was sitting in the grass "covering."

"He's got something!" June cried. "He's got something! And that counts! It's a tie score!"

The boys were grinning. June put her hand under the yellow legs and lifted Zander into the sun. She stared at the prey.

"A grasshopper!" she shouted. "Tie! Tie!"

Her father trotted up behind, looked, laughed, and said, "Wait a minute. I've never seen a grasshopper with so many legs . . . he's got two grasshoppers!"

"Hooray again!" June shouted. "He's ahead!"

"And the winner!" Don said. "It's too dangerous with big prey hunting this field for the small contestant to stay in the race."

"The winner!" Rod shouted and jumped in glee until his knees touched his chin. "Those Indian princes are great. What a bapa!"

June caught up with her father as he walked home. She was feeling expansive. "That was fun," she said.

"The match or the winning?" She smiled sheepishly at his glance. "Junie," he went on, "never feel bad about wanting to win. We'd never get anywhere if we didn't try to excel."

A half-grown rabbit ran out at their feet, and three steps later another leaped off.

"Do all animals leave their parents?" she asked.

"Yes," he answered, "in late summer and fall."

"It's sort of like children."

"Very much like children," he answered, "because we are animals, too."

"Are you going to shove me off your land when the goldenrod blooms?"

"Well, people are a little different. You'll want to go when the time comes. You'll see."

"Never, never," she said. "I *never* want to leave home— I don't think."

And so the summer ended, and the Pritchards went back to school and the regimental life of the city. June studied hard; and that winter her training of Zander made the routine of her study more meaningful, at times even exciting. Her grades were good. And they got better and better. Then one day the school principal telephoned Mrs. Pritchard and announced that he would like to nominate June as an exchange student to Belgium from his school. He would have to have a decision by the end of the summer. Her family was proud and excited. June was excited and scared. That night she held Zander very close as she went to sleep.

10. The Nest in the Meadow

This year June *walked* into the house. She did not run. She helped her mother by carrying suitcases and boxes. On the third trip from the car she stood quietly in the hallway.

"Does the place look any different to you?" she asked her mother.

"No," answered Elizabeth Pritchard, curiously following her gaze. "It is still the same wonderful house at the foot of the mountains."

"But the paper is sort of shabby and dirty, and the staircase looks narrow, doesn't it?"

"Well, the paper has always been shabby and dirty, ever

since I can remember. That's the beauty of the place, and the stairs, well, they couldn't shrink." She tipped her head and looked at her daughter, "Could be those two inches you grew this winter. They've lifted you closer to the shabby wallpaper and farther away from the steps."

"No," June said, "it's something else."

"Well, maybe you really want to leave the dust and narrow stairs and go off to Belgium and see the world and be on your own. *You* have to decide, you know."

"No, please, I can't, I can't." She shook off the idea, and when she looked at the hallway again, it was just as she had remembered it, beautiful and grand.

She walked carefully up the stairs to her room, holding her head high as she had been taught in the interpretive dance class she had taken in the winter.

Another month brought her to sixteen. On her birthday Elizabeth Pritchard gave her daughter a family party. June was generously teased.

"Ho," Don said, "sweet sixteen and never been kissed."

"Or have you been?" Charles jibed.

Her mother tilted her head high and said firmly, "It's none of your business."

June lifted her eyes from the table to her mother's face. For the first time her mother was a friend, not a mother, a friend who made her feel golden and secretive. Today it did not matter whether she had or had not been kissed. Either was her secret. She had earned privacy, and she liked it.

She sat slowly eating cake and thinking about decisions

and first kisses. Then the mood passed. Charles picked up a .22 and went to the front porch.

"A sixteen-gun salute for sixteen years!"

She listened as the blanks went off, felt the blush rush to her cheeks. She ran out across the yard to Zander for protection—and looked down to see that she had attended her sixteenth birthday party in bare feet.

Zander this year was a crime to falconry—he was a pet. A falconer regards a pet as a spoiled indulgence. A pet cannot be a falcon in the grand sense of the name, for a pet cannot hunt, only cry and play. In the spring June had stopped training him, and now he was unable to hunt, but he was free to come and go—like Bobu.

He was not on his perch when she stood under the maple. She whistled and he dove down to her from the sycamore at the creek. He back-winged above her head and dropped on her uplifted hand. He flew to her now, not for food, but out of affection and habit.

As she tossed him into the air and ran down the yard, the bird followed above her, then circled into an elm. She held up her hand. Zander returned. She tossed him into the air, he killied, dove, and swept up the creek.

She ran to the canoe landing and whistled. Down over the water came the falcon. He flashed his wings and alighted on her head. He pulled her hair in his beak.

"You're no lady's falcon anymore. You're a silly American pet . . . and spoiled." June rumpled his feathers. He scolded in irritation.

The change from falcon to pet had come about soon after the invitation to go to Belgium. It began the day June took Zander to an assembly lecture on falconry. The bird flew around the auditorium and came back to her whistle. The high school students leaped and shouted and laughed. She was a gay success.

Then John Doyle, handsome, curlyheaded John Doyle, arose in pensive wonder and said: "What is it about a falcon that makes him able to be trained to hunt, whereas a sparrow cannot be?"

June could not answer. She did not know. She was not embarrassed, but she wondered what the answer was. That night when she put Zander on his perch on her desk and sat down to study she viewed him with new eyes. He was no longer a little person. He was part of the earth . . . and June wanted to know more about him as a bird and why he had evolved to the creature he had become. She opened her drawer and took out a sheet of paper.

"Dear Charles and Don:

How's college? Does Ulysses like German? I have done the worst. I have withdrawn Zander from the Joust. He is no longer a falcon in falconry terms . . . just a biological one. I am sorry, but he is a pet, indoors most of the time. Just the same he is wonderful, and I will never part with him.

Please tell me this. Why does a falcon train to hunt and a sparrow does not?

Don't date the fluffy duffs. Look for a gal with brains.

Love,

June"

And so the falcon and June had finished the spring in quiet companionship as she learned about his feathers and feet and bill and bones and wings. By summer she knew more about birds and sky and what evolution had done to the ancient reptile to get it airborne. The bones were hollow, the breast muscles enormous, the feathers almost piloted themselves, they were so light. The bird was air-lined. This knowledge put her in her place—on the earth with two feet fastened there.

Now, as her sixteenth birthday ended, June put Zander back on his perch, and, softly slipping her feet into her shoes, walked to her room.

The next day Don and Charles were as busy as executives, organizing and packing a secondhand Chevy with camping equipment and suitcases. They were going to drive west for the rest of the summer with a couple of school friends. Finally they were ready and all the Pritchards stood around the car on a cool, dew-lit morning to see them off. Their mother cried. Their father grunted and said, "The food bills will be lower." And June was gnawed by jealousy.

With shouts and waves and hoots they backed out of the yard and drove away. As the dust from the car settled over the nettles and daisies at the side of the road, June sat down on a rock and dreamed of the adventures the four young men would have. She saw the laughing people they would meet—nice, beautiful people. She envisioned the Galahad adventures they would enact—noble, triumphant adventures. And for a long moment she was with them, meeting a handsome gypsy who sang and carried her off with a single kiss to a vague, misty ending.

She sighed. Suddenly back down the road came the Chevy, cutting dust as it rolled up to the house.

"We forgot the cameras!" Don called sheepishly, and jumped out of the car.

Their father came around the house chuckling, "Some planners. You're still little boys." Last year they would have taken the teasing. This year it hurt. Charles grew angry. He flared at his father.

"You forget things, too. How about the fishing rod you left back home?" That was the first time June had seen her brother get angry to their father's face.

Charles senior raised an eyebrow. "Well, you *are* fledging!"

Charles hit back. "What do you mean?"

The slender man rocked back on his heels and said, "The nest is too small."

"It certainly is!" Charles snapped and turned to June as if this break with his father had cleared his mind. "Junie, there's a sparrow hawk's nest in the sycamore tree above the swimming hole. You might be interested in watching how the mother takes care of her young."

She felt uncomfortable but she was fascinated, for Charles seemed to be an adult speaking to a sister who was also adult. "Why should I?" she asked.

"Because," he went on, "it may help you with that question you wrote me at college last winter." He held tight to the cameras and ignored his waiting brother. "Why does a falcon train and a sparrow not? The answer is in the nest, but if you go down there you'll see that we've only elaborated on their wild way of life for our own purposes. A sparrow is a picker, not a hunter.

"And," he added, ignoring his father, "in a way, our trained falcons are forever children. We feed them as if we were mothers. We take care of them, and even though they're physically adult birds, emotionally we keep them dependent fledglings. Go to the nest," he said.

June stood still. As the car drove off she no longer saw romantic gypsies and Sir Galahads. Rather she looked up at her father. She noticed that his hair was thin and the lines around his nose were deep. "Will there be red-tailed hawks for Charles and Don as there were for Zander, Dad?"

"Of a sort," he answered.

"Then why did Charles get so mad at you for teasing?"

Her father smiled pensively. "The time of the goldenrod has come for Charles and Don and me. We'll clash more and more, until, like the young animals in the field, they leave my home and find their own."

"Oh, that's awful," June dropped her head.

Her father continued. "The mother otter turns on her young and bites if they come crying back, the cat spits, the bear growls."

"Oh, Dad," she said. "Not me. Ever."

His arm went around her shoulders, awkwardly. "You'll go too." And he ran his hand over her short, curly hair.

June walked back to the meadow. She located the sparrow hawk's nest and watched the mother come and go for an hour. The female brought food to a limb and tore it in small pieces for her young. She called to her offspring softly.

A head came to the hole and a wide opened beak was filled.

"So what?" she said and went home.

That night she flew Zander over the yard, fed him, and he winged to the chimney top and did not come down.

Darkness settled in, the moths came out. June and her mother went to the living room to read before they went to bed. She had no worry about Zander. She knew he would be on his perch in the morning. The perch was his home.

Early the next morning she went back to the sparrow hawk's nest to see if she could find out more about what Charles meant. If she understood, she might walk up to John Doyle when school started and explain to him why falcons can be trained to hunt and sparrows can't. He would be so impressed by her insight that he would take her flying on ice skates down the old canal, or across the ballroom floor in some white-flowered home to which they had both been invited.

Suddenly John Doyle vanished. The mother bird had returned. She came to the same limb with the same kind of food that she had used yesterday and once more broke her catch into bits, called, waited for a hungry beak to open, and fed it.

The male circled around, screaming at crows, chasing bigger hawks off his property and defending, but not attending, the young.

The third day June went back to the tree. Once again the mother sparrow hawk came onto the limb and broke up the food for the fledglings.

It's just like me and Zander, she thought. I'm Zander's **foster** mother. I offer him bits of food each day, and make him come farther and farther out of the nest—until he flies. He wants food; he comes. I'll bet she makes it more diffi- cult each day to get food until it's so hard, they get their own.

The idea excited her, and she ran home to see if Zander were behaving like the wild ones. He was untethered now and free to come and go. She called, and he plunged down from the chimney where he had been watching bees. He sat on her hand.

She took him to the field and threw him out into the air. He waited on as she kicked in the grass.

A mouse skittered before her. She looked up. Zander did not strike. Instead he went to the apple orchard. There he sat.

"You're out of training," she said. And she left him there. She had promised Emily that she would go swimming.

At dusk Zander returned to his perch. June walked to him to see if he had eaten. He had, for his crop stuck out like a pouter pigeon's.

Once more June went in the early morning to the nest in the meadow. She took a book and stretched out in the warm sun to pass time while she waited to see what the mother falcon would do next.

Presently she brought a sparrow to the same limb, but sat with it in her mouth. She did not break it up but flew to the hole and dropped in the whole bird.

I guess she wants the youngsters to see what they eat, June mused. I guess they learn what they're supposed to catch that way.

Nothing much happened at the nest for two days. On the

third day the female stood on a new limb, far away, gave her funny call, and waited. Two nestlings stood in the door and yelled. It was like Zander's early training period, when she had stood five feet away, then ten feet . . . just like this wild mother. June chuckled ruefully to see that she had not trained her bird at all, just elaborated on his childhood. And the wild young were just as stubborn as Zander.

About an hour later, one of the young in the door could bear his hunger no more. He spread his wings and flew shakily out, scooped the air, and plunged to a limb. He grasped it, teetered, spun, and nearly fell off. His wings and tail balanced him with great spreading movements.

His mother flew to him and rewarded him with a bite.

Then a second bird flew, and another, and a fourth. When they were all out of the nest, the female became nervous and busy as she sneaked among the limbs, feeding her babies, and warning them of weasels and foxes.

The young birds were always restless when they saw their mother. They fluttered madly to tell her where they were, opened their beaks, begged, were fed, and then sat completely still, so still that even with her eyes upon the spot June could not see them when they were full and quiet.

The next day she took her falcon to the field and flew him. Again he did not hunt, just waited on, played, dove, then came down and sat on her head.

June picked him off and threw him into the air. "Go get your own food," she said, and ran across the field. Zander followed. At the road he swooped up into a tree.

That night a storm came up and she decided to bring Zander in. He could find a retreat out of the rain, now that he was free, for his bird sense led him to favorite hollows. But June wanted him to depend on her for at least shelter from storms. She whistled.

He did not come.

She whistled, called, then ran around the house, looking at all the chimneys and lightning rods. He was nowhere in sight.

She asked Rod if he had seen her falcon. He looked up from a map of the constellations he was studying on the porch and said, "No."

She went to bed.

In the morning she was still anxious. Zander was not on his perch. She tried to reason with her anxiety; he had been gone overnight before. She threw a sparrow to Ulysses (she was taking care of him for the twins in exchange for a .22 rifle) and walked out to the field.

She climbed toward the crest of the hill where she could see wide and far. She climbed higher, and looked down. Her heart leaped into her throat, and she felt sick. There, sitting beside the field, was the neighbor farmer with a rifle across his knees.

Shaking, she ran toward him.

"You didn't shoot my falcon, did you?" Her voice trembled.

"Falcon? Falcon?" he said. "Naw, I'm shooting hawks. They get my chickens and ducks. I'm getting rid of 'em."

"But he's a hawk, a little sparrow hawk." She showed him with her hands.

"Oh, yeah. . . ." he said. "That was yesterday afternoon. Gee, I'm sorry—but I only winged him. He flew on."

"Where, where did he go?"

June was crying now, from her head to her toes. The farmer stood up and started across the field.

"Did he have things hanging from his legs?" he asked.

"Yes, yes," she cried. "He did. He did."

"Well, gee, I didn't know he was a pet. You know how hawks are . . . a farmer has to protect his stock. And there are so many of them birds this year that I had to knock 'em down."

They hurried across the field. June wanted desperately to tell him he should not kill the hawks and owls, but no words would come.

They stood at the field edge, among thistles and primroses.

"He was sitting on that dead stub," he said, pointing to a tree in the orchard.

"Yes, of course," June answered. "He hunts the mice that eat your grain from there."

"Well, he was sitting there, and I winged him . . . and, let's see . . . he flopped down about here, sort of fluttering, and I couldn't see where he went so's I could get another shot. I'm sure sorry. I didn't know."

June ran into the grass, whistling and peering behind every plant. She found spots of blood on the leaf of a mullen plant. Her heart beat hard. She called, almost in a frenzy, "Zander! Zander!"

She dropped to her belly and scrambled over the raspberry prickers and through the yarrow and teasel. She searched the brush, ignoring the scratches and thorns.

"Right about where you are," the farmer called.

But Zander was nowhere.

She stood up to let the farmer see if she was really in the right spot, and as she rose her eyes focused higher in the raspberry thicket. There, three feet off the ground, wing clasped tightly to his side, sat Zander. He made a soft sparrow-hawk noise, the noise, June recalled, of the young answering its mother. "I see him," she called. And she struggled into the bush. The bird stepped lightly onto her finger. She grasped his jesses and came back through the weeds to the farmer.

"I found him. I found him," she said, and then, because she could not face the man a moment longer, she tucked her bird in her shirt and ran as fast as she could.

He called after her, "Them hawks is awful on my chickens."

In rage and anger she turned to him. "Well, coop your chickens up!"

Then she was embarrassed and afraid because she had spoken so defiantly. She returned to the yard, her heart beating loudly.

Rod saw the wounded falcon.

"Sors plum? Sors plum? (What happened?)"

Quickly she told him and pointed to the man. Rod put on a firm face and strode into the field.

June turned toward the house and carried Zander to the kitchen where her tears chugged to a stop. Gently she put him on a block of wood by the stove and waited for her father to come home.

The bird sat very still on the post and held his wing just so. He was glad for the warmth of the fire, and gradually lifted his feathers. She left to get some food for him and came back to find him sleeping.

But when she moved, he quickly awakened and grabbed the morsel. He ate it with eagerness and hunger. She stuffed him; he closed his eyes.

June heard the click of her father's car door and rushed to the porch.

"Please, tell me what to do. I think Zander is dying," she blurted.

Her father and her uncle walked together into the big kitchen and bent over the small bird.

"Come on, little fellow," her father said, and picked him up. Slowly he lifted the damaged wing. He studied it, watched it, and softly closed it to the bird's body. His nose, almost under the wing, bent the longest primary feather. Then he said, "We can't put a splint on it. Too high."

But Uncle Paul lifted her spirits. "I was talking to a man who raises ducks, the other day, and he said birds' wings heal in about five days. Said he'd had a duck that broke a wing last month, just crawled under a bush until it healed and then he came out and flew away. His mate brought him food."

Charles senior put the falcon back on his perch. "Junie, I think we should just try keeping him quiet and letting the wing heal without interfering with nature."

"Will he fly again?"

"Well, you heard Uncle Paul. He might."

Her father got some absorbent cotton and some warm

soapy water and gently washed the blood. Suddenly Zander jumped in pain.

"I guess it's best to do nothing," her father said. "He can wash himself in the creek when he's well."

Her mother came into the kitchen. "That's the trouble with pets," she said, "with the joy, there are the heartaches."

The door opened and Brownie ran in. The fast movement startled the falcon and he jumped painfully to the ground.

"I guess I ought to hood him," June said. "Then he'll sit still." She went to the cupboard and returned to slip the little brown hood with the red feathers over Zander's head. He became absolutely motionless.

That night June went up and down the steps a dozen times to look at Zander. Finally she fell asleep. At daylight she sat straight up in bed. A coldness seized her. She knew Zander was dead.

She bolted downstairs and with stiff movements opened the door.

The bird was sitting exactly where she had left him, his wing held so that it would heal. She sat down beside him and said softly, "Hi, little fellow." In the darkness he heard her voice and lifted his feathers. The small noise of the nestling greeting its parent came from his throat.

After breakfast she checked him again. This time she did not fear he would be dead; limp and sick, perhaps, but not dead. So she laughed with relief to see him sitting perkily on his perch, standing quietly under the hood.

She went to the meadows and came back about ten, confident that she would see Zander better. She was getting used to the idea that he would live.

The next morning she was anxious but not afraid.

Three days later she went back to the sparrow hawk's nest in the meadow.

She watched the mother bird and her young, now hidden on branches and behind leaves. They were hard to see except when they fluttered their wings to attract their mother. It was a slow game, and once again June lay down in the grass to watch them. As she stared up into the tree she suddenly realized she was looking at one of the puffy, pinfeathered, bespeckled fledglings. It was a male, clinging tightly to a limb, just as Zander had clung to her shirt the day her brothers brought him home.

As she watched, the fledgling puffed until his head and body were a round ball. Suddenly the feathers flattened. The head lifted, the wings fluttered. His mother was coming. She must have been far out in the sky for it was many moments before she flashed onto a near limb. The young bird stretched to her. He fluttered like a Japanese fan. She sat still with food in her mouth. The fledgling flapped toward her. Her wings went up. She fell backward off the limb, spread her finger-feathers, and rolled out on the sky.

She carried the food with her.

The youngster dove after her. And then she turned and struck him! He fluttered, zigzagged to a tree, and perched recklessly on a twig. His heart was beating so hard his body shook, his beak stood ajar.

June remembered her father. "She doesn't want him," she said in awe.

The young bird sat alone for a long, long time. Then he jumped to earth and caught a tiny cricket. He ate it. He watched the sky. He beat out the "here I am, Mother" call, but the mother bird did not answer. He rotated his head from horizon to horizon as he followed his mother's flight. She never came back.

"That's horrible," June cried; and for no reason she could find, tears ran down her face.

"It's just as Dad said, he's being sent out into the world to seek his fortune. His mother won't help him anymore. It's horrible to live in the wild. It's frightening and cold and awful. I'm glad I'm a person and don't have to go to Belgium if I don't want to."

At home Rod was on the canoe landing checking his star map with a reference book. The door opened and her mother stepped out. She was in her bathing suit ready for a swim. June was glad to see her.

"I'll swim with you," she called and sped to her room. She stopped in the kitchen and looked down at the bird in the hood. He was fluffed and warm and still. He heard her presence and gave the soft call of the fledgling.

"Are you feeling better?"

Zander stretched, pushing one foot and the good wing down, down in a line together. Then he shook—and lifted *both* wings into the air.

June spun to his side. Carefully she removed the hood and put her finger behind his feet. He stepped upon it, looked at her and then at the room.

He focused on the door, the highest perch—where falcons like to be. June waited breathlessly to see if he would fly; knowing he couldn't, hoping he would. Slowly he extended both wings. He gently beat them, testing their strength. He beat deeper and deeper . . . until he taxied above her finger. He stayed in the air an instant, flapping evenly, and then dropped back. He was tired, and flew to his perch.

June kicked open the screen door.

"He flies! He flies! Zander flies again!"

Rod called, "Hooray!" He came grinning to the kitchen, "Now maybe you'll help me find the double star in the Dipper tonight."

"I will. I will."

Just before dinner June heard a soft knock on her door. Her mother came in with a letter in her hand, an invitation to a dance to be held next month.

"It's from the group that is going to Belgium. An Albert Reed wishes to take you. Do you want to go?"

"Oh, no, no," she said. "I despise him—he's a stupid intellectual—and besides, if I accept the dance it means I'm going to go to Belgium—and I don't want to!—There's my modern dance class—and Zander. Who'll take care of Zander? I just can't go!"

Her mother looked at June steadily, moving her head slightly to the left. She seemed to be checking June almost the way she checked her jelly—waiting for two drops to come together to form something solid.

"All right," she said, and knew the kettle should bubble some more.

I I . *The Bolt of Organdy*

The house seemed to be full of noise. Aunt Helen spanked
"Rustles of Spring" out of the old piano, and Rod was call-
ing June to come look at an enormous map of the Northern
Hemisphere. Above the din June heard the alarm call of
Zander, "killie, killie." It came from the top of the house.
She ran out the back door to see in the sky—another spar-
row hawk.

She remembered Windy, and that far fix in his eyes when
he had flown off. She picked up an apple and threw it to
divert Zander. It fell to earth, but as it did the movement
caught his eye. Then he saw June. She whistled and called

and whistled. He flew in close to her in the apple tree. He would not come to her hand. She had to climb the tree to bring him down.

For the first time in many months she tethered him to his perch. The other sparrow hawk in the sky was a female. It was not the mating season for sparrow hawks; some birds that lose their mates while raising young often go out and find another. No widow was going to lure Zander!

Zander fought the leash, and then resigned himself to the shady perch beside Ulysses. Ulysses was all nobility now. People came from far and near just to see the kings' bird, head high, chest out, eyes black, patched and beautiful.

June spoke to Zander as she tethered him. "You've been catching most of your own food lately. I've got to feed you both now," she said. Ulysses lifted his feathers and bowed to her as he might bow to a mate. "But, I'd sooner do that than have Zander go off with some silly female."

The falcon larder was low. She went to the house for the .22 and lured Rod into going with her to the barn. He brought the bird net in case the sparrows were flocking in the hayloft.

At the barn they met the farmer who had wounded Zander. He was working at some enormous task involving a bowl and many small paper cups.

"How's your little bird?" he asked as they entered the barnyard. June reported he was quite well again and flying around. Then Rod asked him politely, to make conversation, what the cups were for.

"Poison," said the farmer. "I'm just overrun with rats and mice. It's terrible this year. They've nearly ruined my granary and they're getting into the barn now. I gotta poison them before I starve."

"Do you think," said Rod testily, but trying not to be rude, "that it is because you killed all the hawks and owls that were killing the mice, that now the mice are so many they are forced into your barn to find food?"

"Well, I don't know about that," he said. "I don't understand all those wild things, but I know what has to be done. I gotta kill rodents."

Rod said, "May I suggest you stop shooting the hawks and see if the mice disappear?"

"That's crazy, boy," the farmer said. "I've farmed all my life and I *know* what devils the hawks and owls are. They take poultry by the dozens. Why they got three of my chicks in one night. And I'm gonna shoot them every time I can."

Rod did not argue. He would leave the persuading to his father.

He and June climbed to the hayloft where they could hear the hundreds of sparrows that were besieging the farmer. Rod said, "I think I'll be a teacher when I grow up." He took one end of the net and walked across the yellow-green hay.

June looked at him, slender, eager, handsome. "It seems you have to unteach before you can teach, like the farmer. Plors clay? (True?)"

"No," he called back. "Mr. Miller is right in the middle of a great big lesson. I'd like to be the kind of teacher that finds the Mr. Millers in the world and demonstrates that nature's balance has been changed by shooting the hawks and owls. Then Mr. Miller would see it himself. I think that would be exciting." Clutching a beam with one hand he held up his side of the net with the other. He said slowly, "Even more exciting than inventing a new language."

June fastened her end of the net to the other side of the barn, then walked across the hay, circling around a flock of chirping sparrows.

She whispered across the dust, "Rod, that language was wonderful."

"Aw, it was silly nonsense," he smiled. "I've even forgotten most of it."

The stubble scratched June's legs and the hot air of the barn dried her throat and eyes. She looked at Rod.

"Oh no, you must never forget the language."

"Yes, I must; it's done. Like a broken toy—pooh, you toss it away."

June was aware of the resonant pitch of Rod's voice. Impulsively she asked, "Did the language go when your voice changed? Is it part of your squeaky days? Have you outgrown it, Rod?"

"I guess that's about it." He thought a moment, then said, "The other day when I shaved a little bit I could not remember how we declined the verb 'to be.' Funny thing."

"I hope you become a teacher, Rod," June said softly, and bravely "shooed" the birds. Six flew into the net and were caught. They took the birds home without more words.

That night she carried Zander to her room. There she held him under her chin trying not to cry over the lost language.

For three days she kept Zander tethered. The fourth day she set him free. He killied and winged around the yard, displaying his feathers and yellow feet. He was a spectacular sight. She laughed and was pleased that he was hers.

With a flick of his wings he dove on a large black cricket, and proceeded to swallow him whole. June dropped onto her knees and snatched the cricket from her bird.

"No, you don't," she scolded. "If you catch all your own food you'll go wild. I'm not refusing to care for you like the mother in the sycamore!" She scratched the bird between the eyes. He leaned into the movement and closed them in pleasure, as funny noises came from his throat. June jumped up and ran to the icebox for food. Zander was on his perch. She held the food out. He spanked the air with his wings, snagged the sparrow, and sailed to the chimney with it. Anxiously June watched him devour the food high above the house.

"Now, you come back," she called.

Two days later Zander disappeared again. June tried not to think about him the first day, but the morning of the second she met Jim seining in the meadow and asked if he would help her look for her falcon.

They whistled and walked far across the meadows and fields. Jim found other sparrow hawks, wild ones; he found a young crow, and the eggs of a turtle. Finally he said, "You don't think he got any of the mice Mr. Miller might have killed with his poison? Dad said that some of those poisons can kill the bird that eats the mouse."

June spun to look at him. "Oh, Jim, you don't think . . ."

They were almost to the mountains. June turned and ran
. . . over the yellow mass of butter-and-egg blossoms . . .
all the way back to the house. She whistled and called as she
leaped the hedge and sped to the barn.

She boldly walked to the farmer's house and knocked on
the door.

"Have you seen my falcon around here?" she asked.

"That thing again? No. But a screech owl fell dead right
out of a tree beside me this afternoon. Plunk. Dead. Odd
thing."

"What did you do with him?"

"Oh, I tossed him on the compost heap back of the
chicken house. Wanna see 'im?"

"Yes. May I?"

"Sure, help yourself." He pointed the way.

June knew what she was going to see. Her brothers had
brought Bobu with them to Pritchard's one day during the
past winter, and Bobu had flown out of the car. They could
not wait for his return, so they asked a neighbor to try to
catch him. When they came back the following weekend
the neighbor reported having seen him every day on the
sleeping porch of the Pritchard house, his new red jesses
marking him from all other screech owls. School children
said he had waited for their bus in the evening and then
followed them to their yards and porches. But nobody could
get near him.

Then he disappeared completely in January and was not
seen again.

One day in June, Uncle Paul saw bright red jesses on an
owl near the barn. It was Bobu, carrying food in his beak.

"By golly, that means he's got young," he laughed, and returned to tell the boys. They were happy for old Bobu. Rod wondered if his children turned in circles.

As June walked to the compost pile, she thought about the owl's new home on this farm. But she went on—all the long, long way to the chicken coop, and around it. She stopped at the sweet pile of grass and leaves.

On the very top was a red jesse.

As June walked into the yard she saw Jim reading the funnies. She told him. He turned away and lifted his hands to his face. In the house her mother was sweeping the parlor, Aunt Helen was playing the "Intermezzo" from *Cavalleria Rusticana.* June blurted out her news.

"Bobu is dead. He must have eaten a poisoned mouse."

Rod heard from the living room. He folded his star map saying, "I ought to get more A's in school so I can go to college and become a teacher. I do want to tell about the controls in nature. Poor little Bobu."

Then into the silence June cried out, "And I know Zander has been killed by the poison, too! He's gone!"

"Oh, not necessarily at all," her father said calmly as he came to hear the news. "He would much rather eat grasshoppers this time of year than mice. I think his own inner timing and delicate taste has kept him very much alive."

"I hope so," she said.

But the next day he was not back. June said nothing more about Zander, just whistled and looked at the treetops. It was a long, tense day.

The next morning her mother urged June to come to

market with her. They shopped and poked and bought shoofly pies and scrapple and home-smoked hams. They smelled flowers and apples and lingered over the intricate crocheting done by a little Amish lady. Then they crossed the street to the same old brown department store. Her mother wanted to buy a pattern for a skirt.

June still hated that store. She walked awkwardly through its aisles as they went back to the yard goods counter. But when she passed the underwear department she was surprised to see that it was a very tiny part of the store. She remembered it as enormous, and she realized how young and silly she had been two years ago.

Suddenly her eye struck a beautiful color—yellow, cool, bright and fresh. It was like clear daffodils. It was a bolt of organdy. She touched it. She turned the bolt over and moved along the counter. Her mother stood beside her.

"That's lovely, isn't it?" she said. "It would make a beautiful formal dress."

"Oh, it would!" June could see the organdy gathered in bright folds, and the folds falling around her slippered feet. Everyone was staring at her as she tiptoed across the beautiful living room at the Bunkers' and twirled endlessly with John Doyle.

Her mother snapped her out of the dream as she unrolled a yard and held it against her face. Suddenly it all seemed too real to June. She pushed her mother's hand away. ". . . but I don't need a formal. Goodness!"

"Well, you ought to have one. There will be lots of things coming up this year, and you don't always find material when you need it. If you like this. . . ."

And so they bought yards and yards and a pattern with a pretty bodice and rolling skirt. June was excited and thrilled but at the same time somewhat resentful. The dress meant parties and "being a lady" and left hands in laps, small steps, deference to elders—it meant all the rules— and more.

But the color was heavenly and she opened the bag wide on the way home to see how sunny the yellow was. Suddenly she said, "What did *you* want in the department store? We got so excited about the organdy that we forgot what you went for."

"Oh, I can get it next week," her mother replied. "It isn't important."

"Are you trying to make me forget Zander?" she asked.

"No! No, I'm not. It's just that a formal dress follows sixteen the way three follows two."

June helped unpack the car and put away the foods, all but a cupcake which she sneaked to the porch to eat. As she bit into it she looked up to see Zander on his perch! "Oh, bird!" she cried and ran to him.

"That settles it!" she told him, "no more freedom for you. It's unfair to let a pet who trusts mankind fly free among men who want to kill him."

She snapped the swivel in the jesses, "There!" Her mind was made up. She wanted her falcon.

For a week Elizabeth Pritchard made tiny French hems in the yellow dress, and June watched her hands flash and dip as she took dainty stitches. June did not offer to help, for she was angry at the whole idea. Toward the end of the week Charles senior picked up the gown and held it awkwardly before him.

"Hmmmm, it's nice," he said.

June turned her back and walked to Zander's perch. She threw him a maple key. He snagged it with his orange-yellow feet and bit it playfully.

"You must not go away," she said. "And I won't either —even though I feel a hand on my back."

That night Rod taught June some of the constellations. He had studied his subject well, and June found it thrilling to bend her neck and look up and out and out into the sky. The no-limit of it, the endlessness of the speeding universe, made the top of her head open and she knew what it was to be outside herself.

As she leaped off the earth, she said to Rod, "Can you really think that there is no end out there?"

"I can think it," he answered, "but I can't visualize it."

"It's crazy," she said, "stars beyond stars beyond stars forever with no end. It's impossible to even *think* it's true . . . except, I guess, for those people who make new languages."

He chuckled in the darkness and pointed out the Corona Borealis. "You liked that language, didn't you?"

"I still do," she answered.

Each day June fed the tethered Zander a sparrow—until the goldenrod yellowed the roadside, and the twins wrote that they were on their way home. And each day she wandered and moved aimlessly, wondering what she was all about and what life would bring her.

And then came the morning her mother called her to fit the dress. June resented having to try it on, but her mother had worked hard on it, so she obeyed.

"Oh, well, I'll try it on . . . I'll never wear it, so why worry," she said to herself.

Elizabeth Pritchard was a seamstress with a flair. She loved to sew. At the fitting she put the dress on inside out, took a tuck here, let out a dart there, and then pulled the whole thing off.

"Do you like it?" she asked.

"I guess so; but it's full of pins and seams and it's hard to tell." June hated herself for her petulance, but she could not control it. The beautiful dress and its adult world frightened her.

The next afternoon was sunny and bright. June took a book to the creek to read, but stopped on the way at Zander's perch. He looked so beautiful—his rusty back, blue wings, black eye patches—that she wanted to be near this exquisite bit of art she owned. She stretched out on her stomach and opened her book.

Three pages later she unsnapped the falcon's leash. He was free. She held up her hand. She whistled. Zander flew to her. She put him back on his perch, held up her hand, whistled. He flew again, skimmed her fingers and winged into the ash tree. She leaned on her elbows and called. Zander lifted his head and killied, killied—a fierce bird. Then he dove up into the air and feather-landed on the chimney.

He was back on his perch at suppertime.

She brought him in for the night and in the morning

opened her screen to let him fly out. "I'll leave it open, so you can come and go as Bobu did," she said, more to herself than the bird who was becoming so independent.

At noon Zander alighted on her head as she came home from the fields with falcon food. She put him on her fist and said to him, "I really like you to be free. You know the rules. Just don't abuse your freedom. I want you near."

She threw him into the air, listened to his wings rustle, and was glad as the light flashed from his white undercover feathers.

At lunch there was a letter from the boys. "And then at a carnival in Catchem, Wyoming (of all places), two men came up to us and said, 'Please help us out, and change our luck by putting our last fifty-cent piece on a number.' We felt sorry for them because they explained that they had been betting all night and had lost. They added that they would split the money with us if they won. Don put the fifty cents on black twelve . . . and won! . . . two dollars. We didn't want half, but they insisted and said, 'Well, why don't you fellows bet it?' We did. And before we knew it we had lost ten dollars, at which time we realized they owned the concession and had really taken us in!"

June was horrified. "Is that what people do to young men out in the world?" she asked, and Elizabeth said with a chuckle, "Well, they learned a lesson—and a cheap one at that."

"What did they learn?"

"To judge people a little better," she said smiling, glad that the world had not juggled them too hard—just enough.

That afternoon Zander came fluttering over June's head.

She jumped, snatched his jesses in the air, and tethered him. She did not know why.

The following day Emily ran into the house, brown-legged and smiling. June was making a fish casserole for supper. The table was set and it was time to feed the falcons. Emily's hair was wet from swimming and she sparkled.

"Junie, there'll be a school band concert tomorrow night. My sister and brother and two friends of his are coming. That leaves an extra boy . . . would you come too? It will be fun with rides and booths and tenpins to knock down."

Emily's sparkle shone on June. "I'd like to," she said brightly, "but don't let anyone give you a free throw." And she told Emily about her brothers out in the West.

The Band Concert was gay and pleasant, and the next morning while she fed Zander she unsnapped the leash to remove a kink from it and the falcon pulled out of her hand and flew to the roof of the house. She whistled once, then left him, for Emily ran into the yard to talk over the exciting moments and people of the evening before.

Zander was gone for three days.

The fourth day he came back to the yard, but did not fly to her hand, just sat in a tree above her and waited until she climbed to him. Then, just as she reached him, her foot slipped; she spun on the limb, scared Zander, and he winged to the rooftop.

He was gone all day and all night.

The next morning from her window June saw him in the sycamore by the creek and called, "Come back, Zander." She whistled. He did not fly toward her so she started down the back steps to climb the tree and get him.

She was at the head of the stairs when she heard her mother call, "Junie, the yellow dress is finished! Come try it on."

With one foot on a step she started to say, "Just a minute." But the words didn't come out. Instead, she turned and walked into her mother's room where the thread was being ended in the last mile of hem. Her mother shook the dress and held it up. It was cool spring, white slippers, waltzes, stars.

June fought down her desire for it.

Then hesitatingly she took the dress and held it to her. It smelled new. Her head ached on the very top, as, hugging the dress, she ran into her room where the wardrobe mirror hung. She thought of the white dining rooms at the Bunkers', of glittering candlelight in Belgium, and of laughing, whirling people.

She pressed the dress against her body and looked at her golden reflection. As she did, she saw Zander in the mirror. He had winged into the willow tree that grew beside her roof. She needed only to reach out the window and she would have him. She would do that.

But first she turned slowly before the glass admiring the dress for its yellow beauty, afraid of what it meant, hating its inevitableness, and yet living its breathlessness. When she had completed the circle the falcon was gone.

She ran to the window, threw up the sash, and leaned far out. The beautiful, beautiful sparrow hawk was circling the chimney. His eyes were focused on a far spot in the sky. He arced over the slate roof, tilted his brilliant wings like signals in the sky . . . and waited on. June made no move. She made no call, no whistle.

Zander circled the yard, the stream, the fields. His course widened. He faced east, dipped his wings in steady rhythm . . . and was gone.

She turned from the window and clamped her fingers over her face. She would never see her falcon again. Into her curled hands she whispered, "Good-bye, Zander, good-bye. How different the winds will be that carry us." She waited for the tears to break and fall upon the yellow organdy.

But no tears came.

The enthusiastic reception young people accord each new book by Jean George is seconded by their parents, teachers, and by librarians. Many of them agree that her works are destined to become classics in children's literature. *Dipper of Copper Creek* (written in collaboration with her husband, John George) received the Aurianne Award for the most outstanding animal story published that year. *My Side of the Mountain*, published in 1960, affirmed again her remarkable sensitivity to the often interrelated worlds of child and animal life.

Mrs. George, a native of Washington, D.C., received her B.A. degree in English from Pennsylvania State University. She has held the position of art editor for *Pageant Magazine* and has served as a newspaper reporter for the *Washington Post* and International News Service. She is a regular contributor of nature stories to *Reader's Digest*.

Mr. and Mrs. George and their three children live in Chappaqua, New York.